CASE FILES O...

A METHOD TO MADNESS

BY

JUDITH WHITE

World Castle Publishing

World Castle Publishing
Pensacola, Florida

Copyright © Judith White 2012
ISBN: 9781938243561
First Edition World Castle Publishing May 15, 2012
http://www.worldcastlepublishing.com

Licensing Notes

Cover: Mark Nemecek
Editor: Maxine Bringenberg

DEDICATION

I'd like to thank Bobby Kuzniar, for without him, Sam Flanagan would not have been created. To Bridget Frankhouse, I give my thanks and love for all her support in being my sounding board. To Charlene Partlow, I give my appreciation for her enthusiasm and support. And last, but certainly not least, I give thanks to my husband, Jim White and my children, Brandon and Erin. They listened through writes and rewrites and encouraged me to continue, telling me I could do it.

Charlene,
I love you & always will!
Judeeth White
5/30/12

Judith White

CHAPTER ONE

In my line of work, you never leave the job until it's finished; or rather, it never leaves you. You eat it, drink it and sleep with it. And sometimes, after the case is long over with, the story still lives on in your soul. This was one such case.

It occurred in the winter of 1943. I was a private detective, and after the solution to this puzzle was discovered I carried all the what ifs and whys around with me. The guilt of not being able to prevent a death haunted me; it probably would for the rest of my days, however many I had left. I felt as though I had unwittingly played a big part in helping to carry out the tragedy—and I didn't like that. I didn't like the idea of being put in the position of…well, I'm getting ahead of myself here.

Because I craved crime—to solve it, not to commit it—I was a cop on the Detroit police force. From 1933 to 1937, I called the department my home. But because of a couple of scrapes I found myself immersed in, which I am not going to go into right now, it was decided by my commanding officers that we should amicably part ways. It wasn't that I wasn't good at what I did for a living; I was. Let's just say there were certain rules, a lot of red tape, etc., that one had to follow and I didn't do that. I'm rather bull headed in the fact that I see things *my* way, and that's the path I felt I needed to follow. The force didn't see it the way I did. If truth be known, though, I missed being a part of all of that; the camaraderie with the other officers, the excitement and adrenaline of always having a case to work on, and I certainly missed a regular paycheck. Thankfully, I still kept in contact with a couple of the guys I had worked with; at least I had that.

In the months following my departure from the department, I opened up my own private detective agency. It was eighteen days after Christmas, January 12, 1943 and I sat in my office, pondering my life. Being in need of money and action, I didn't have a case; nothing was brewing. So I watched the activity—or in this case, mostly the *in*activity—of Woodward Avenue from my second story window. Snow was falling lightly, but steadily, and I wondered if the roads were going to be slick. I was playing with a rubber band, twisting it around my thumb and forefinger repeatedly. In the background was the music of Glenn Miller's *In the Mood*, emanating from a small radio I kept on top of my filing cabinet. I was thinking about the fact that I'd be turning forty this year. (It's funny how the days merge into weeks and the weeks roll into months and the months turn into years and, all the while, you don't notice how quickly it's passing.) I was thinking about Dee Dee, my former wife.

We'd only been married four years, but they were a good four years, at least I thought so. She couldn't quite get the dreams to evaporate from her mind and soul, though. She'd dreamt of Hollywood and stardom and headed west, leaving me behind. That was a good ten years ago, right before my induction into the Detroit Police Department. I thought of her less and less with each passing day, but when she did come to mind, I still felt a bit of sharpness within me. She used to tell me I had Hollywood eyes, whatever that was. It must not have been a bad thing, because she never said it condescendingly.

Physically, I was nothing spectacular, but I would say I was not unattractive, either. I suppose I was just a bit on the good side of average. I stood six feet two inches tall and weighed approximately two hundred and seven pounds; well, I weighed that a year and a half ago, which was the last time I'd checked. I didn't believe I'd changed all that much since then. I had black hair and blue eyes—what was typically referred to as black Irish.

The ringing of the telephone on my desk startled me and the rubber band shot from my hand, hit the window, and fell to the floor. I turned in my swivel chair and picked up after the second ring.

"Flanagan Investigations," I said into the mouthpiece.

"*Huh*? Who *is* this?" asked a voice speaking very loudly into my ear.

"Gran?"

"I'm looking for Sam Flanagan!" she blared again. "Is he there?"

"Gran, it's me. It's Sam."

"Oh, who was that other fella who answered the phone? I thought you worked alone."

"I do work alone. That was me who answered the phone," I explained.

"*Huh*?" she yelled.

"What did you want? I'm on the phone now, so just tell me what you want."

"You're on the phone now?"

"*Yes*!" I bellowed, a bit more impatiently than I should have.

"Well, dear, you don't have to yell," she said. "I didn't mean to interrupt your call. I'll try back later."

She'd hung up before I could protest. My grandmother's confusion was humorous, yet annoying. I rolled my eyes toward the ceiling and started slowly counting aloud. *One…two…three…four…*I reached thirteen before the phone rang again.

"Flanagan Investigations, this is Sam Flanagan speaking," I said loudly, clearly, succinctly.

"Sam? Is this you?" she asked.

"Yes, Gran, it's me."

"Well, I think you'd better get home here," she said.

"Why? What's happened?"

"The mail has come, dear. I think we received something important!"

She was still shouting. Ruby Flanagan failed to realize that when speaking into the telephone, she didn't have to bridge the distance with a raised voice. She also looked forward to seeing the postman approach the house each day. Whether it was a bill to pay or an advertisement from the local five and dime, she thought it might be important and would make me read it to her in its entirety. She couldn't perform this simple task on her own because her eyesight had been failing her for years.

"Can't it wait for a bit? I'm at work. I'll come home in a little while."

"Are you working on a case?" she asked.

"Not at the moment," I said and sighed.

"Well, then why can't you come home now? And when are you going to get a real job?"

"I'll be home later, Gran," I said. And I hung up.

I'd moved in with my father's mother right after my divorce. She was alone, I was alone and it seemed the sensible thing to do. I'd been living with her ever since, and while it presented no problem for the most part, every once in a while it felt confining.

I bent down and opened the bottom drawer of my filing cabinet, taking out an almost full bottle of Jack Daniel's whiskey and a glass. I poured myself two fingers and turned back to the window. My gaze focused on the *Handy Hardware* across the street. No one was entering, no one was exiting. Things were slow all over. It was times like this that Gran's words rang loudly in my ears; *when was I going to get a real job*? When I was in between cases, never knowing when the next would appear on my doorstep, that's when I considered switching careers. But this was in my blood—I couldn't deny that.

I downed my whiskey and figured nothing was going to happen today, so I might as well head for home before the roads became too dangerous. I started to get up from my chair, but slumped back down as my door opened. The first thing I saw was her legs. They were stunningly perfect. I had a hard time tearing my eyes away from them. She walked in and sat in the chair opposite my desk.

"Are you Sam Flanagan?" she asked in a tone that was businesslike.

"I am," I said.

"I want you to follow my husband."

My gaze traveled north. To be honest, her legs were her best asset, but she wasn't unattractive by any means. I figured she was in her very early fifties. Her hair was a deep shade of brown, and hung in loose curls around her shoulders. Her eyes were framed at the outside by a feathering of soft lines; creases a bit deeper had begun to form at the corners of her mouth. She must've been beautiful once, say about ten or fifteen years ago. I zeroed in on the eyes. She had one gray and one blue. *Amazing*, I thought. The closest I'd ever come to seeing an abnormality like this was back in the third grade when Koots Johnson had a big patch of solid white hair on the crown of his head. He and his family moved away after that one year and we never did find out why his hair had turned white in that particular spot, nor did we learn if his first name was really Koots or if that was just a nickname.

"I want you to follow my husband," she repeated herself.

"And why is that?"

"You don't know who I am, do you?" she asked, changing course all of a sudden.

I shook my head and said, "Why don't you tell me, sister?"

"I'm Phyllis Killburn."

I didn't react.

"Oh, for heaven's sake! I traveled hours from Chicago to see you."

I still said nothing, wondering if I were missing something that was supposed to be right in front of my face. Maybe she was off her rocker...some dames her age were.

"Phyllis Killburn? From Chicago?" she persisted.

"Okay, so you're Phyllis Killburn from Chicago. Should that mean something to me?"

"Oh, for heaven's sake! What did I expect?" she sighed with disgust. "Mr. Flanagan, my father was Alden Whitaker!"

It didn't register in that split second after she told me, but then a light bulb went on in my head.

"*Ah*!" I said. "*You're* his daughter? You're *that* Phyllis Whitaker?"

Alden Whitaker was a staple of Chicago high society. He *was* Chicago, or at least *had* been until about four years ago. He'd come to the city from parts unknown with a dream and made it happen. At the age of forty-seven, back in 1913, he became the sole supplier of tires to the Ford Motor Company in Detroit. He'd made a fortune and hobnobbed with the finest in politics, business and entertainment. He'd been part of the cream of the crop. Four years ago, at the age of seventy-three, he'd suffered a fatal stroke, leaving all his riches, I'd assumed, to his only child, Phyllis.

"Yes, I'm *that* Phyllis Whitaker…well, Mrs. Phyllis Killburn now. I want you to follow my husband, Mr. Flanagan."

"And just why is that, Miss Whitaker…uh, Mrs. Killburn?"

"Because I think he's involved with someone else. Isn't it obvious?"

A Method to Madness

CHAPTER TWO

"Okay, so why don't you tell me what makes it so obvious to you?"

"Well, there have been some calls lately that he's rather secretive about. Some nights he stays away and doesn't come home at all. I just have this feeling, Mr. Flanagan, that he....well, that he...." Her voice trailed off.

She leaned down to pick up her purse. She set it on her lap, opened it and withdrew a white handkerchief that was edged with lace, then dotted her eyes with it. Was she crying? It was hard for me to tell. I said nothing and allowed her time to compose herself.

"I guess you'd say it's woman's intuition," she finally said.

"Well, sure, I can look into this if you'd like. What does he do for a living, Mrs. Killburn?"

I asked all the normal questions about his activities. Some of her answers didn't sit well with me. She told me that he played the piano at a lounge downtown some nights, and that he was also connected with the military, but she didn't know in what capacity exactly. She told me that she didn't want to know. That threw me for a bit of a loop.

"Are you saying he does work in military intelligence?" I pressed.

She lowered her eyes and twisted the handkerchief with her fingers. She didn't answer right away—I didn't push her.

"I'm afraid to know what he does, and he doesn't talk about it. Or won't," she whispered.

"But you think it's something dangerous, don't you?" I asked. "You think he might be spying for the government? Passing secrets along? Something along those lines?"

"I don't know!" her voice raised a notch in frustration. "Oh, I shouldn't have come! I'm sorry I wasted your time."

She started to rise from the chair, but resumed sitting when I held a hand up.

"Now hold on," I said. "Let's calm down a bit. You came in here because you think he's seeing another woman, right?"

She nodded, looking into her lap. I made a deal with her that we would just focus on the possible affair; we'd leave the other business alone for now. She agreed—then opened her purse again, withdrawing an envelope stuffed with cash. She placed ten one hundred dollar bills on my desk and asked if that would be enough of a retainer for me to get started. I made a throaty sound and tried to cover it with a cough.

"That'll do," was the only thing I could think of to say.

"There's a dinner party coming up on the twenty second that I'd like you to attend. There are always dinner parties, Mr. Flanagan. The high ranking military officers that my husband deals with will be there. I can have a car pick you up if you'd like."

I told her I would let her know. My mind was still reeling from the large amount of money that was in front of me.

She reached for a pencil and piece of paper that were sitting on my desk and quickly jotted down her home phone number, telling me I could reach her there when I'd made my decision. Then she got up to leave.

"Allow me." I reached the door before she did and opened it, letting her pass, and watched her legs carry her down the hall to the elevator, savoring the sight. She hesitated and turned to me before pushing the button, appearing to want to add something to what she'd already told me. But she didn't say a word. She turned back and hit the down button, and then she was gone.

I stood for a moment more, eyes fixed on the elevator, leaning against the doorjamb of my office. What did I know about this case? Next to nothing. A dame shows up claiming to be Phyllis Killburn, nee Whitaker. She claims to be married to a guy who is stepping out on her and also claims this said guy is heavily involved in the military; but as to exactly what he's doing, she doesn't know and he doesn't say. I had no idea if her suspicions were correct as to his cheating or to the military intelligence angle. Okay, we *were* in a nasty war, trying to fend off the aggression of the dirty rotten Nazis and Japs. It was plausible—hell, even probable—

that the old man was doing some patriotic work for his country. And then a chill of fear ran the length of my spine. What if, assuming he *was* in the spy business, it wasn't for *his* country? What if *he* was as dirty as the Nazis and Japs? Sweat formed along my brow and under my armpits. This had me frazzled. Maybe I was way out of my league on this one. Maybe I'd better forget this little scenario and stay here; not make that trip to Chicago. Maybe I'd better—

The opening of the door to the office next to mine roused me from my musings.

Oliver Treadwell emerged with all his photography equipment balanced under his arms, on his shoulders, and in his short, midget like hands. His bald head was smooth and shiny and his glasses had fallen precariously down the bridge of his nose. He was startled at seeing me halfway in the hall.

"Oh! Mr. Flanagan! I am so glad to see you!"

He let all of his equipment slide graciously and carefully from his grasp and to the floor.

"I have an errand for you, if you would be so kind," he said.

He made a beeline for me in his short, quick steps while reaching into the inside pocket on the threadbare suit jacket he wore. He extracted a white envelope, standard sized.

"Will you please hand in my rent at the end of the month?"

I stared at the envelope as he passed it to me.

"Sure, Ollie, but you can't do it?"

"Oh my; heaven's sake no, Mr. Flanagan. I'm on my way back to St. Louis to photograph my new born niece."

He beamed with the pride any new father would display.

"Ah, so your sister had the baby, huh?"

"Yes! Day before yesterday, and she named her after me!"

"Ollie?"

"No, silly. Olivia!" he said impatiently, as he shoved his glasses back into position.

"What about the newspaper?" I asked, inquiring of his work. He freelanced at the Detroit News and maintained a private office here in the building.

"I'm not the *only* photographer, Mr. Flanagan. They can get along just fine without me for a couple of weeks or so."

He turned suddenly and started to balance his camera equipment again. He pushed the down button to the elevator as I backed into my office and closed the door. I made it behind the desk and to the window just in time to see Mrs. Phyllis Killburn exit the *Handy Hardware* carrying a bag. She entered a waiting, running, shiny black 1942 Ford Super Deluxe. Nice! It was the only car manufactured by Ford the previous year due to the war effort. As for Mrs. Killburn coming out of the store, I found that to be odd. It didn't seem right to me. Buying something in a hardware when she could've easily sent her man in? A very rich woman in her early fifties in a hardware store: what could she possible have purchased? I watched as the sleek, expensive auto slowly headed south on Woodward Avenue and drove out of sight.

I sat down, mindlessly turning the envelope in my hand, thinking about my trip to Chicago. There was no way I was going to be picked up by her driver. Old Chi Town, The Windy City...and then it hit me! Harold Blevins!

Harold Blevins was an old classmate of mine who had gone on to be an investigative reporter for the Detroit News. He was a lot like me in that he didn't play by the rules. They had given him the boot after only five years on staff there. As luck would have it, he'd gotten a second chance when the Chicago Tribune had offered him a position eight years ago. He and his high school sweetheart, then wife Annie, had moved to the big city, and I was thinking of the possibility of staying with them. My friend would probably be a great source of information for me. We'd lost touch shortly after his move, but old friendships never die, right? At least I hoped that would be the case this time.

I opened my top drawer, reaching for my keys, and was about to throw in the rent envelope when I stopped suddenly. I stared at the blank white paper and thought, *oh, what the hell*! I already had the stack of hundreds in my pocket, but who knew how much this little jaunt was going to cost me? I ripped open the envelope and withdrew three tens, thinking, *This might come in handy*. But as I pocketed the extra cash, I felt my blood rising, my anger mounting. I was ticked! Oliver Treadwell was being charged $30 a month for rent while yours truly was paying $32.50! I'd have to put dealing with that on hold. Right now, I had a case to work on.

I tossed the envelope in the trash, gathered up my coat and hat and left the office. As I locked the door, I heard the phone ring from inside. No doubt it was Gran again, worried about the unread sale papers. I'd deal with that, too, when I had the chance. I was going to buy her the strongest reading glasses I could find.

Judith White

CHAPTER THREE

The snowfall was increasing and so was the ferocity of the wind. I pulled my collar up closer around my neck as I stood outside of the building that housed my office. Looking across the street, I decided to make one more stop before heading for home.

The hardware store had only one other customer, a slight, stooped man in his seventies. He was being helped by a man who might have been the owner. As they talked over plumbing equipment, I meandered throughout the aisles, looking at nothing in particular. I kept wondering what Mrs. Killburn could've been doing here. What had she purchased? It was probably of no consequence whatsoever, but I was curious. I looked toward the front of the store and out the window onto the street, wary of how bad the weather was becoming.

That's when I noticed a handwritten sign that read *Authorized Arms Dealer*. *Hmm, that's interesting*. I spotted the counter that displayed the firearms and headed toward it. When I'd left the department, some six years ago, I naturally had to leave my weapon behind. I'd replaced it, of course, but the newer gun never felt right in my hand. I hadn't used it much, and that was a good thing, but I always wanted to get something more comfortable to the touch. I heard the cash register clang with the old man's purchase and raised my head just in time to see the clerk, the owner, whatever he was, heading my way.

"Howdy! Help you with somethin'?" he asked in a friendly manner.

"Just looking," I replied.

I bent my head, eying the different handguns in the case.

"Is that what I think it is?" I asked, pointing to one model in particular.

He slid the glass door open on his side of the counter and reached for the piece I'd indicated.

"If you're thinkin' it's a German Luger, you'd be right," he said, handing it over for me to hold. "The wife's nephew brought that back with him. He wasn't over there three months before he came home with his shoulder all shot to hell. Told me he took it off a Kraut he'd killed. I don't doubt he picked it off a dead Kraut, but what I *do* doubt is that he did the killin'. You'd have to know him; never was much good at anythin'. But if he's willin' to tell tall tales, I guess I'm willin' to sit and listen to him. I told him I'd try to sell it for him. And actually, it's the best bang for the buck among these."

"Why's he selling it?"

"Ah, he's fallen on hard times. He's takin' care of a wife and mother-in-law and now he's got a kid on the way. Can hardly keep a job with that bum arm of his."

The gun felt good in my hand and I liked the way it looked. The stories I could tell about it was an added feature. I told the man to wrap it up along with two boxes of ammo and handed over the cash.

"Boy, this is his lucky day. I sold the other one he brought back today, too," he said, as he handed me my change.

"No kidding! He brought back two of them, huh?"

"Yeah, and I sold the other one today to that skirt that walked across from your buildin' not more than a half hour ago. You do work across the street there, don't you? I see you goin' in there most every mornin' and I figure you work there."

"Yeah, I work there. Well, you take care now. And thanks." I took the bag from him and turned to leave. I held up my purchase as a gesture of goodbye.

"No, thank you!" he called as I passed through the door and into the cold once again.

Once inside the '38 Chevy, I started the engine and let it idle, trying to fill the interior with heat. That was odd. Phyllis Killburn had bought a German Luger. How did she even know the hardware had carried weapons? What was her intent in purchasing it? I doubted she was a collector. I didn't like the sound of it at all. Maybe there was more to the story than she'd told me. A woman didn't shoot her husband for only suspecting a betrayal— well, most women didn't. She might have been holding back on something. Was she really *that* afraid of the line of work he was in? Did it have something to do with the espionage angle? I now knew one thing...I wasn't going to wait around until that dinner party to go to Chicago. I had the rotten feeling in my gut that I had better get there as soon as possible.

****

When I pulled up to the house, I saw the two boys from next door playing some type of war game in their front yard. The older of the two, Albie, was a good kid, but could be annoying at times, always asking me to pitch ball with him, or build a snow fort, or something. He was about eleven or twelve years old and had a father who couldn't be bothered with such things because that would take time away from his drinking. His younger brother Bobby was probably eight years old, and as talkative and outgoing as Albie was, Bobby was just the opposite. I didn't think I'd heard him utter a dozen words in all the time I'd known him. I was trying to figure out a way to get past the two boys when an idea came to me.

"Hey, Albie! Come here a minute."

He ran over to me with eagerness.

"Yeah, Mr. Flanagan?"

His brother was right behind him and was now staring up at me through brown horn-rimmed glasses. His eyes were squinted and his nose was crinkled.

"How would you like to earn some money?"

"Sure! Doin' what?"

"I have to go out of town. I'll be gone for about a week, maybe more. I want you to come over and read the mail to my grandmother while I'm gone. Can you do that?"

"Sure," he said. "But I have to go to school first."

"By the time you get out of school, the mail should've already been delivered. How's your reading?"

He shrugged his shoulders and replied, "Purdy good, I guess."

"Pretty good will do."

I reached into my pants pocket, took out a dollar bill, and handed it to him.

Reaching for it, he said, "Wow! A whole dollar!"

"Just remember, if I find out you didn't do the job, I'm going to ask for that back," I warned.

Bobby hadn't taken his eyes off me and was still staring at me now. I pulled out another fifty cents and handed it to him.

"And that's for you. Your job is to make sure Albie does his job."

He nodded silently and excitedly before running at lightning speed toward his house, where I assumed he was going to show his mother what I had given him. I sure as hell hoped he wasn't going to show his father. He'd never see it again if he did that. He'd be contributing to his father's whiskey fund if the man ever caught wind that I'd given the boys money.

Gran wasn't too thrilled about my trip to Chicago, and to be honest, I wasn't too thrilled with leaving her for a stretch of ten days or possibly more. I told her I'd call her every couple of days or so, and I also let her know about my deal with Albie. I handed her twenty dollars and told her to go easy with it. She tucked it in the top of her housedress and inside her brassiere.

After a quick bowl of her homemade chicken soup and a couple of biscuits with butter and honey, I packed a bag and headed for the Greyhound station. I didn't relish the thought of taking the bus, but on the way home from the office I had noticed an ominous clank somewhere under the hood of the Chevy. Not good! I wasn't going to chance the 300 miles or so, and especially not in this weather. I'd have to drive it to the station, but I would leave it in the lot, locked up. In the past the auto had served me well, and it still had a long way to go before I could afford a newer model.

Apprehension always filled me when taking on a new case and this time it was no different. I felt out of sorts. What was I walking into, if anything? What would greet me in Chicago? I had no idea if Harry and Annie still lived there. The Chevy was worrisome; hopefully, it wouldn't cost me an arm and a leg to repair. And my biggest concern was about Gran. I was uneasy about leaving her, and for that reason, I was beginning to doubt taking on this case. Quite possibly, I had allowed the sight of all those bills tossed across my desk to cause me to make a hasty decision.

CHAPTER FOUR

I wanted to get a window seat on the bus, so I made sure I was in line to board early. I hated traveling this way, but what else could I do? I boarded the bus behind only one other passenger; a tall man of about 400 pounds. He wore a brown suit, brown tie and brown hat. The rim of his hat was dotted with sweat as it poured down the sides of his face. He carried his top coat folded over his arm and close to his chest, and his labored breaths echoed off the walls of the vehicle. He wedged himself in the third row behind the driver, choosing the aisle seat.

Passing him, I went back two more rows and climbed in on the same side, but right next to the window. I started to rise again and move further to the back because a foul odor coming from him wafted toward me, but it was too late; people were in the aisle taking their seats. Slumping back down, I vowed to wait it out. If I were lucky he would be exiting the bus in Ann Arbor.

I caught the eye of two young men dressed in military uniforms. They sat across the aisle from me, sitting side by side. I nodded and they nodded back. When everyone was settled, I turned to them.

"Shipping out or returning?" I asked.

"We're being sent out Monday. Going home for a few days first, sir."

"Chicago?" I asked.

"I am, sir," the one sitting in the aisle seat responded. "Earl, here, is from Kalamazoo." Earl leaned forward and nodded. I nodded back.

"Where to?" I asked again.

"Not sure. Could be anywhere, sir."

Earl leaned forward again and said, "Anywhere we can kill Nazi's or Jap's, sir. That would be my wish."

I understood. We all fell silent except for my occasional cough and sniff from the acrid odor hitting me in the face from big boy two rows up. The last thing I remembered was seeing a road sign indicating Ann Arbor was six miles ahead.

I awoke when the bus came to a stop at the Jackson station. I straightened, a bit dazed from sleep, and wiped the drool from the side of my mouth. Both boys in uniform were dozing across from me and softly snoring. Unfortunately, the human blimp was still among us. He was sleeping, too; exerting loud gurgles with every breath.

The bus driver announced we had a twenty minute wait until we continued on our journey. We could stretch our legs, get coffee or use the facilities. I decided to do all three. When I returned, I carried three coffees, passing two of them to the soldiers. In less than a week's time they might not get a good cup of java for who knew how long.

It was 8:18 p.m. when we arrived at the Chicago Greyhound Station, meaning it was 9:18 p.m. back home. The place was much larger and more crowded than the station in Detroit. I looked for a telephone booth and found a group of them along one wall. Unfortunately, all were surrounded by people waiting to use them. I got in line. When I finally gained access, I quickly looked up Blevins in the phone directory. There were eighteen of them in Chicago: only one Harold A.

I dialed the number and got a busy signal. *Damn*! I disconnected and dialed again. Hearing the same signal, I hung up and then gave it a third try. Someone pounded on the glass behind me and the noise caused me to jump.

"Come on, buddy!" a deep male voice shouted.

The busy signal still sounded in my ear. I hurriedly glanced at the address accompanying the phone number and committed it to memory.

"It's about time, Mister!" the same man yelled as I walked away. I found a group of cabs out in front of the station and went to one. Leaning down, I stuck my head through the window to talk to the driver.

"Can you take me to 214 E. Oakland Street?"

"Sure can. Get in."

I slid in the back seat and he pulled away from the curb and into traffic. He looked in the rearview mirror at me.

"That's not too far from here. Wanna take a cruise around the city first? Do a little sight seein'?"

"Nope."

I could hear him try to stifle a sigh of disappointment. He was trying to build his fare but he'd have to make up for it with the next sucker.

****

The house was a small white—or used to be white—bungalow, badly in need of a fresh coat of paint. Houses only lined one side of the street; on the other side was a set of railroad tracks.

I carefully approached the few steps to the miniscule porch. No one had shoveled in many days of snow. The screen door hung precariously on its hinges and it creaked when I knocked on it. I heard an angry male voice shout from inside.

"Myra! Myra! Get the damn door!"

Myra? Well, son of a gun! I should've told the cabbie to wait until I'd made sure this was the Harold Blevins I was looking for. Damn it! Now what was I going to do? Maybe there was a little Myra, an addition to Harry and Annie's family I knew nothing about? I could only hope.

The door was opened by a petite, sort of frail looking woman, probably in her early thirties. Her dark auburn hair framed a face that could be pretty with a bit more care and make up. Freckles dotted her cute, up turned nose and cheeks, and there was a small greenish bruise on her right cheekbone at the end stages of healing. The apron she wore over her housedress was spotted with stains and grease. She was very pregnant—and she wasn't Annie! Oh boy! She looked at me with questioning eyes. "I'm sorry," I muttered. "I was looking for Harold Blevins—Harold Blevins who works at the Chicago Tribune—but I see I have the wrong house."

"Well, who are you?" Her voice was childlike.

"I'm Sam Flanagan, a friend of his from Detroit."

She broke out into a smile that lit her eyes.

"Hey! Well, sure, he's talked about you! Come on in. Yes, come on in."

She reached for my hand to pull me into the warmth of the house.

"Harry! Harry! You just ain't gonna believe this!"

Harry was looking bad—unshaven, hair going this way and that, and half in the bag. He held a half-empty glass of amber liquid. He squinted when we entered the living room. Surprisingly, the house was immaculate. A brown sofa, a brown print chair, two end tables and a coffee table were dust free. A radio sat silent near the sofa. In the far corner was a small portable desk with a covered typewriter on it, along with a small desk lamp. It was obviously a place of work for Harry. Recognition transformed his face and he jumped up, sloshing his scotch.

"Hey! Why, ya old somabitch!" He slurred.

"Hey, Harry." I extended my hand to shake his. "How ya been these days?"

He shook my hand loosely and fell back in the chair, spilling more of his drink on his undershirt. He wore black pants, a sleeveless undershirt and no shoes or socks.

"Have a dring wit me." And then turning to Myra, who was sitting next to him on the arm of the chair, he said, "Ge' 'im a glass."

She started to rise but I put my hand up and stopped her.

"No. No thanks, but tell you what. You got some black coffee? I could use some strong coffee."

Before she could get up, Harry roughly poked her and told her to go fix the coffee. He was a little too disrespectful to this woman for my liking. He caught my look of disapproval. When she was out of earshot, he leaned forward, and nodding in the direction she'd gone, said, "She'sh my wife," as if this gave him the right to treat her poorly.

"Your *wife*?"

"Yeah, Annie's been gone three yearsh nah."

He closed his eyes and tossed back the rest of his drink. I took the empty glass from him and set it on the table.

"Tell me about it," I said as I sat on the couch, leaning forward with my elbows on my knees. I figured I knew the reason she'd left him, if his behavior tonight had anything to do with it. But she hadn't left him. She'd been shopping downtown in December of '39 when a car came speeding around the corner she was attempting to cross, killing her instantly.

"The somabitch never even shtopped. The bassard kep right on goin'."

He looked around for his bottle of scotch. I grabbed it before he did.

"Nuh unh. No more. I gotta talk to you about a case and you're no good to me like this."

Myra came in carrying three cups of coal black coffee, and I told Harry to drink up.

He'd taken two sips of the hot fluid when he suddenly jumped up and headed for what I assumed was the bathroom. From the sound of it, he was emptying a month's worth of stomach content. Myra turned to me.

"He ain't a bad man, Mr. Flanagan. He just gets to where he can't handle things, I guess. He told ya 'bout Annie?"

I nodded that he did.

"Well, he gets a bit sad at times. I knew her, too. She was the best friend anyone could ever want. I loved her, too."

"He do that?" I gestured to her cheek. Her hand came up to cover it and she looked embarrassed.

"Please don't be mad at him, Mr. Flanagan. He don't do this offen. He don't really hit me 'less he's really feelin' bad."

We heard the shower running and in another ten minutes a new man joined us. Harry was dressed and his damp brown hair was combed straight back. He looked human again.

He kissed his wife gently on the forehead and whispered an apology in her ear. She blushed and took her coffee to the kitchen to leave us to talk.

"Sorry, Sam. Now what's this about a case?"

I told him everything I knew in regards to what Phyllis Killburn had told me, which wasn't much. I ended with the information I'd gotten from the hardware store owner about selling her a Luger. He shrugged and told me it was possible that Eddie Killburn was messing around, but he'd never heard anything around town about it. In fact, he'd never heard anything negative about Eddie Killburn at all.

"Look, we ran their engagement announcement. I should have a copy of that issue of the Trib around here somewhere. Hold on."

He left the room and I waited.

The announcement was dated March 15, 1941. The headline ran:

Whitaker Tire heiress to wed

Miss Phyllis Calvert and Mr. Edwin Killburn
will exchange matrimonial vows on
September 12, 1941 at two o'clock in the
afternoon at the First Methodist Church of
Chicago. The celebration, immediately
following the ceremony, will take place at the
private residence of Wilmer and Iona Cosgrove,
longtime friends of Miss Calvert. Seventy-five
people are expected to attend. The couple will
then enjoy a ten-day honeymoon in
Mexico City, Mexico.

Miss Calvert, longtime resident of the city,
is the daughter of the late tire tycoon, Alden Whitaker.
Edwin Killburn, calling Chicago his home for
the past year, hails from Buffalo, New York.
Our best wishes to them both.

I then studied the three photos that accompanied the brief article. The first was of Phyllis, but underneath it again stated her name was Phyllis Calvert. This was the dame alright, but she appeared much younger; maybe fifteen or twenty years younger than when I saw her. In the picture, her eyes were brown, both of them. The second photograph was of a young, handsome man with wavy black hair combed away from his face. He appeared to be about thirty years old. His broad, winning smile displayed white, even teeth. He had a dimple in his left cheek. The third was a photograph of Phyllis and her father, Alden Whitaker, attending some sort of charity event in London, England. King George VI, accompanied by his daughter Princess Elizabeth, stood beside Phyllis and her father. It had to be one of his last trips out of the country before his death. This had me puzzled. Why use such young photographs of the couple? And where did the name Calvert come from? I scratched my head and voiced my confusion to Harry.

"She wanted us to use a younger photo of her and wanted us to fix the eyes…make them match. Now this picture," he said, pointing at Eddie Killburn's image, "was very recent at the time this article came out. He's got to be twenty or twenty two years younger than his missus."

A low whistle escaped my lips. I looked at his photograph again. He really *was* a handsome guy; as Dee Dee would say, Hollywood material. I couldn't help but wonder why he chose Phyllis. I would stake my life on the fact that he could've had any much younger female that he had wanted. Maybe there *was* something to her fears of his seeing another woman or even other *women*, for that matter. Maybe he only married *mama* for her money in the first place.

"Okay, so tell me about this," I said, pointing out the name of Calvert.

"Oh, she was married some twenty or more years ago to a guy named Jack Calvert. They secretly got married by a priest here in town and it lasted a whole five months. I don't know why she kept the name. Anyway, daddy didn't care for the situation so he made sure it ended. Seems Jack wasn't too scrupulous and kept company with the likes of one Al Capone."

I whistled again. Things were becoming a bit clearer. In the days ahead, I hoped they would become clearer still. I could understand now why Phyllis Killburn had her suspicions, and I could see where buying the Luger fit in. That scared the hell out of me.

CHAPTER FIVE

Myra graciously offered me their home for the night, and for as long as I was in town. I put up a bit of a fight, but not too much. I needed a place to stay and didn't want to spend the money for more than a week in a hotel room. I also didn't have transportation, so this was perfect.

She brought out a pillow and blanket and told me the sofa would have to do for one night. Tomorrow she would see to it that their spare bedroom would be ready for me. Lights were out at the house just after 11:30, and I laid in the darkness of the living room thinking about Phyllis and her husband. I still couldn't get over the fact that Phyllis had married such a young man. She must've been around fifty-two years of age and he looked about thirty. Actually, my real surprise was in *his* marrying *her*. I didn't doubt her suspicions were valid, and her fear of him might not be all that farfetched. I am not sure how long I laid there mulling over what I had learned before drifting off to sleep, but morning came all too soon.

"Sam. Sam, get up. Breakfast is almost ready and I thought you could go into the Trib with me this morning."

I opened my eyes to see Harry standing in the living room looking at me. He was showered, clean-shaven and dressed. I grunted in response so he would know I was fully awake. He left the room and I swung my legs to the floor. Running my fingers through my hair, I longed for another couple of hours of sleep.

I emerged from the bathroom after showering and felt a bit more energized; it was 7:45. After a meal of scrambled eggs, bacon, toast and coffee, Harry and I walked out to the garage at the rear of the property. Inside, two cars were parked. One was a brown 1936 Plymouth Sedan and the other, a black 1929 Ford Model A. Harry tossed me a set of keys.

"Sorry, buddy, but you get the Ford to drive while you're here. Thing is though, I haven't had it out in a while, so I want to have Duke check it out when we get to the Trib."

"Duke?" I asked.

"Yeah, he's the best mechanic in town. Too bad he's a copy boy at the Trib. Follow me."

He got in the sedan and started to pull out, and I followed.

The Chicago Tribune was located on W. Washington Blvd., not too far from the city hall building. Harry pulled into an adjacent parking lot and I was able to park right next to him, even though the spaces were filling up fast.

"She run alright gettin' over here?" he asked.

"I didn't notice any problems."

"Good. Still want to have Duke check it, though. Hey, Sam, I've come up with an idea. I'm going to introduce you to my editor as a reporter from Detroit. That way you'll get a press pass. You might be able to get into places easier while you're here."

"Sounds good to me," I said.

The Chicago Tribune was already abuzz with activity when we entered. From the greetings that Harry received, I could tell he was well liked and well respected. I could tell he was regarded as a seasoned reporter. In that moment, I felt proud of him.

An older man emerged from a door that had 'Editor in Chief' stenciled on the top glass portion. He started walking our way.

"Mornin', Charlie. I want you to meet a friend of mine—works for the News over in Detroit. Sam Flanagan, meet Charlie Kuntz."

He welcomed me by shaking hands and asking me about Ty Carver.

"How's that S.O.B. doing these days?"

I felt a heat run through my body. I had never heard of a Ty Carver before, but I suspected he must be Charlie's counterpart at the Detroit News. I swallowed my fear and told him that Ty was doing just great. He accepted that and asked no more questions, thank goodness.

"Charlie, I was thinking Sam might be able to get a press pass while he's here. He's workin' a story."

"Of course he can, boy. Get one off my desk." Turning to me he said, "Good to have ya around,

Flanagan," and then he headed toward the break room with an empty coffee cup in hand.

Harry made a couple of calls from the phone on his desk in his cubicle, one being to Duke, and then went into the editor's office and retrieved the pass. Handing it to me, he told me to follow him.

"I want to show you something." he said, leading me out of the building and toward the parked Plymouth. We got in and he pulled out onto W. Washington again. "I want to show you where you'll be going for that dinner party a week from Saturday," he explained.

I sat quietly, taking in the sights of a city beginning its workday. The only other time I'd been to Chicago was with my father. I'd been maybe six years old when we made the journey, just the two of us, to visit his brother, my Uncle Roan. That was the last I ever saw of my uncle. He worked in construction and some five years later, while on a girder eight stories up, he'd fallen to his death; he was only thirty-six. I'm sure the city had been quite a different place back then.

I should've been paying attention to the direction in which we were heading, but I wasn't—I was too engrossed in the sights and the people. Harry slowed and pulled over to the curb and parked. We were on N. Damen Avenue. He nodded to an establishment across the street.

"That's it. That's where she's been giving dinner parties for years."

I leaned forward and looked to my left, past Harry, so I could get a better view. A large marquee above the door read *Violet Hour* in purple lettering. The entryway was a set of heavy wooden doors with round porthole windows in each. On either side of the doorway were gigantic cream-colored marble pots that, in better weather, would hold flowers or some type of green foliage. It looked elegant; it looked posh.

"One of Capone's haunts," Harry said.

"Huh?"

"*Violet Hour*. Capone used to hang out here back in the day," Harry repeated.

"No kidding!"

"Yeah. I hear he's not doing too well these days."

"Who? Capone?"

"Yeah," Harry said. "He's down in Florida and word has it he's not a well boy."

He turned to look at *Violet Hour* again and said, "Holy Moly, speak of the devil!"

I turned, expecting to see Al Capone entering the club, but instead, saw Phyllis Killburn and a man exiting the double doors. I'd seen this man before. It wasn't her husband, Eddie. I watched as they made a right turn and walked away from us along the street. Her step was quick and her arms were wildly gesturing. She was talking, more like ranting, to the man. Phyllis Killburn was definitely in an agitated state.

"Wow, wonder what that's all about," Harry said.

"I don't know," I said, still watching them. "But I need to know who that guy is."

Harry turned to me. "I don't know his name, but I know what he does. He's one of her drivers. He's her bodyguard, her gopher, so to speak. Why? You think you recognize him?"

41

"He's the big guy that was on the bus from Detroit with me," I stated.

CHAPTER SIX

Harry was about to start the auto when I put my hand on his right shoulder, stopping him from doing so.

"Hold on. I want to go in there for a minute."

"What do you expect to find out?" he asked.

"I don't know," I shrugged. "Probably nothing. At least nothing to do with this case, but I'm curious. I shouldn't be long."

"Want me to go with you?" He offered, but I shook my head no.

Traffic on N. Damen Avenue was a bit busy and I had to wait for seven cars to pass before I could cross the street. The heavy wooden doors opened into an inner foyer. Inside that, two more heavy wooden doors to the right led to the interior of the establishment. It was beautiful inside. The carpet was a thick, plush, solid plum color. The walls were a warm shade of cream and were graced with gold framed scenic paintings. Four crystal chandeliers hung from an ornate ceiling. I wondered what the rooms looked like where one would throw dinner parties, because this was just the lobby. They had to be fabulous. I could see why the Killburn's would choose *Violet Hour* to entertain their guests.

"Can I help you, sir?" A man asked in what I thought sounded like a phony British accent. The words were deliberate and drawn out. He stood behind what reminded me of a reception desk in a fancy hotel. Looking to be in his mid-sixties with a gray toupee badly planted atop his head, he wore a black suit with a white shirt and a black and silver diagonally striped tie. I quickly flashed the press pass Harry had handed to me.

"Chicago Tribune," I said. "We heard that the Killburn's are throwing a bash a week from Saturday and we want to cover it. What time and what's it for? Is it charity?"

A young man in his early twenties, dressed exactly as this gentleman, was standing at the other end of the reception desk and appeared to be writing in some sort of ledger. As he continued his work, he started to snicker. The older man shot him a dirty look and loudly cleared his throat. He turned back to me.

"You heard *wrong*, sir. There will be no dinner party of the Killburn's *here*."

"Ah, I get it," I said. "Trying to keep it under wraps, huh? Must be some big affair then?"

"I assure you, sir, there *is* no big affair! Now I must ask you to leave."

He started to come from behind the desk to escort me to the door. I got in one more question before he reached me.

"Then how come I just saw her leave here with her boy in tow?"

Junior was too stupid to have taken the previous warning and blurted, "Well, if she'd pay her—"

"*Delbert!*" the man shouted. "*Enough!*"

Delbert hung his head lower and resumed writing. The older man put the palm of his hand onto my back and guided me to the door. I left without further irritating him.

"Well? What'd you find out?"

"Nothing much."

I told Harry about the conversation in *Violet Hour*, ending with Delbert's indiscretion.

"Wow, I've never known her to have an affair anywhere *other* than this place. Okay, let's see if we can figure this out. What could he have meant? 'If she'd pay her *bill*.' 'If she'd pay her *tab*.' 'If she'd pay her *dues*.' It's not like she doesn't have it to pay. What else could it be?" Harry asked.

I shrugged. "Doesn't matter. Who cares? The thing is, it has nothing to do with *Mr.* Killburn and that's who I was hired to find out about. That," I nodded my head toward *Violet Hour*, "didn't tell me if he's got a dame on the side or not."

I turned away from Harry and looked out the window and sighed. He started the car and pulled away from the curb. I thought we were going straight back to the Trib, but Harry turned down an alley about five minutes away from *Violet Hour* and told me he wanted some coffee and a Danish. I didn't argue. It sounded good to me, too.

****

The back of *Ma's Diner* opened onto an alley where the parking was tight. Harry let me out before pulling into a space. I could've waited for him, but I didn't. I made my way between the diner and a gas station to enter from the front. I looked at my watch, noting it was close to lunch time. No wonder the place was packed. The tables and booths were all taken, but I spotted two seats at the end of the counter and sat down. I removed my hat and set it on the stool that was next to the wall, saving it for Harry. I sat down on the one to the right of it, right next to a guy who had to be close to eighty.

He was mainly bald, but the hair he did have was like cotton candy, swirling around his head in long wisps. He was wearing a tattered raincoat in which the left pocket was ripped away from the coat itself, and was just hanging by a few threads. It was worn thin and couldn't possibly be much protection against the wind and cold. A cup of coffee was on the counter in front of him. He wasn't drinking it, but rather, was searching his pockets for something. He was having a rough time of it, though, because of the fact that he was shaking severely. I thought maybe he was sick, but then I caught a strong whiff of whiskey coming from him. He kept searching and, finally, came up with two steel pennies from his right pocket and laid them on the counter. Then he stood to check the pockets in his pants.

I turned around, looking out the front window of the diner in search of Harry. Where was he? What was taking him so long? When I turned back, the guy was still rummaging through his pockets in hopes of finding more coins.

"What'll ya have, Baby Cakes?"

The waitress was tall, gray haired and wrinkled. She was also loud, and was furiously cracking her chewing gum. Her nametag read Linda, and she had her pencil poised over her order pad.

"Uh, I've got a friend coming, but we'll have a couple of coffees when he gets here."

I caught her eye and discreetly nodded toward the old gentleman. I said in a low tone, "I'll pay for him. Put it on my bill. You got something you could feed him? That'll go on my tab, too."

She immediately turned to the old man. "Gus. Gus, honey, sit down and don't worry about it. This guy's gonna foot the bill. He says you should eat. Whaddya want, Hon?"

Geez! She talked so loud; it reminded me of my grandmother. I rubbed the palm of my hand over my face. This was exactly what I was trying to avoid. I didn't want to cause embarrassment to the elderly man. Now half the diner was looking at Gus, as if he was some sort of curiosity. Gus didn't answer. He turned to me and he seemed confused. But she continued.

"Want some eggs, Gus? Or how about some chicken soup?" she blared.

"Just bring him the soup!" I said, sharply. I was irritated.

"Sure thing, Baby Cakes." And she walked away.

I didn't know if Gus would've preferred eggs over the soup, but I'd always heard from my mother and grandmother that chicken soup is good for what ails you, and this guy had a heap of ailment. I turned in my seat again; still no Harry. What on earth?

47

I'd no sooner faced forward again when Linda was setting the soup in front of Gus, who had managed to hop back up on the stool. I heard the door open and saw Harry enter, but before I could question him as to what caused his delay, he ran to the corner telephone on the wall behind me. I couldn't hear the whole conversation, but I heard the end of it.

"Just do what I told you, Annie! Tell your sister to come get you and take you to your mothers." He slammed the receiver down and took his seat at the counter.

"What was that all about?" I asked.

"Tell you later."

He seemed out of sorts and out of breath. Something was bothering him, but I let it slide. He excused himself to go to the men's room, telling me to order him a piece of peach pie along with his coffee. I told Linda to bring two coffees and two pieces of the pie.

Before she went to get our order, she made a spectacle of Gus again. The fellow couldn't quite get the spoon to his mouth because of his tremors and had opted for picking the bowl up to drink it. He wound up spilling half of it down the front of his already filthy shirt.

"Oh, for God's sake, Gus! Looky what you done!"

All eyes were upon him again. She mopped the front of his shirt with her hand towel.

Had she not been a woman, I would've jumped the counter and decked her.

****

When Harry returned he seemed less agitated and more like himself. The pie was delicious…I didn't think

48

anyone could make crust like my grandmothers, yet this was just like hers. We were halfway through our pie when the noise of some type of argument floated through the dining area from the kitchen. I couldn't tell what it was about until the involved parties came out and were behind the counter.

"That's twice now this week, Jacko!" the older, heavier set man yelled. "I can't afford for you to be late. You either get here on time or you don't have a job!"

"But it wasn't my fault, Benny! I swear! I was comin' in the back way when someone come up behind me and biffed me one. Knocked me out clean cold. Look… look at the back of my head."

He leaned down so his boss could see the damage.

"Well, no more, you hear me? No more bein' late or you can kiss your paycheck goodbye!"

Benny went back into the kitchen and Jacko leaned down to pick up a bus tub containing dirty dishes that was under the counter. He looked up and that's when he saw me.

"Hey! You! You're the one who biffed me back in the alley!"

"Whoa, now, Jacko. Wasn't me. I've never seen you before."

"But you were in the alley. I seen ya walkin' toward the street."

"So? But the guy who slugged you was behind you, right? That wasn't me."

He had to think about that one—it had him confused. He walked in the kitchen, bus tub in hand, with his eyebrows furrowed.

I'd noticed when the argument came out into the front of the diner that Harry had picked up a menu, pretending to read behind it.

"So what'd you slug him with?" I asked in a low tone, eyes focused forward.

"Hey, I thought he was following you. He was moving like a bat out of hell. I thought he was after you."

"Uh huh." I said, still not looking at him and talking out the corner of my mouth. "So, tell me. What'd you slug him with?"

And Harry, keeping his eyes looking straight ahead, picked up his coffee cup, took a sip, replaced it in its saucer and quietly said, "A tire iron."

CHAPTER SEVEN

Back at the Trib, Harry sat at his desk going through messages he'd received. I sat in a nearby chair, rubbing the back of my neck, trying to work out a headache that was coming on. Last night the sofa was comfortable enough, but I was awakened by a large rumbling noise from a passing train on the tracks across the street around 3:30 a.m., and didn't sleep well after that. I was beginning to feel the effects of that now.

Harry looked over in my direction. "You alright, Sam?"

"Yeah, just a bit of a headache. Harry, I need to ask you something. At the diner, when you first came in, you made a call. Well, I hope I'm not overstepping my bounds by being too nosy, but who was that to?"

"Myra, why?"

"You called her Annie. When you were talking to her on the phone, you said Annie." He slumped back in his chair, running his fingers through his hair and sighed heavily.

"Aw, damn it, Sam! What she must think of me?" he said in an apologetic tone. "I just get to thinking about Annie, and well...I don't know. I had a dream about her last night and..." His voice trailed off.

"I just thought I'd mention it."

"Thanks, Sam. I'll have to watch that. Myra's a good woman and I *do* love her," he said, as if trying to convince me.

I nodded in response and he started to laugh.

"Seems all so silly now," he said, looking at me. "The call to her, I mean. That Joe I knocked unconscious this morning; I thought he was tailing you and I couldn't be sure he hadn't seen me. I didn't know what we were dealing with. If he *had* seen me, I didn't want him coming after me and getting to Myra, especially in her condition." He laughed again. "I told her to call her sister to come pick her up."

I laughed right along with him.

"Well, one thing's for sure. Jacko's headache has to be a lot worse than mine. By the way, I *did* notice her condition. When's the baby due?"

"Mid-March." He radiated with anticipation and pride and I smiled.

Harry picked up a pencil and threw it up in the air, catching it again. He tossed it back on his desk and picked up the stack of messages.

"Well, I've got to follow up on these leads or I'll be out of a job. Wanna come along?" I declined, telling him that I'd like to speak to his editor to see if he knew anything about Phyllis and Eddie Killburn that would help me fill in some pieces.

"Good idea," Harry said. "But before we go our separate ways, let me make a call to Duke first." As he dialed, he asked, "Think you can find your way back to the house from here?"

"Yeah, I think so."

I could only hear Harry's end of the conversation.

"Give me some good news, buddy...oh, that's great...yep, yep, I owe you one. Catch ya later and thanks again."

Harry rose from his seat and reached for his overcoat and hat. He turned to me.

"Well, you're all set. He says the auto is in good running condition. Guess I'll see you later at the house."

I made my way through the pressroom toward Mr. Kuntz's office. After a quiet tap on the editor's slightly opened door, I was hailed in.

"Ah, Mr. Flanagan, what can I do you for?"

"Got time to talk? I'd like to ask you about something."

"Sure, come on in and sit a spell."

I moved into the office, pushing the door shut behind me. He had two black leather chairs opposite his desk and I sat in one. Charlie Kuntz, Editor in Chief, had the whitest hair I'd ever seen. I pegged him to be in his early sixties. The man was short and stocky but appeared to be very solid. He had a jolly face and I couldn't help but think he would be perfect playing the part of Santa Claus at the local orphanage each Christmas. Leaning down, he opened a drawer and withdrew two large shot glasses and a bottle of Kentucky bourbon. He held up the liquor in a silent offer, and I nodded. Filling both glasses, he slid one to me across his desk. I took a sip and admired the smoothness.

"Very nice!" I said, holding up the glass.

He tapped the bottle with a forefinger. "*This* is the good stuff, boy. My buddy down in Louisville ships it to me a few times a year."

Before I could mention what I wanted to talk about, he continued.

"So you say old Ty is doing well, eh? I haven't seen him in quite some time."

I cleared my throat and coughed into my fist. I was beginning to sweat a bit and it wasn't from the bourbon.

"Uh, yeah, yeah. He's doing well."

"Well, ya know how he lost that eye, don't ya?"

"Oh sure, everyone at the News knows the story."

I was wishing he'd drop the subject of this Ty Carver. I didn't know the guy and I felt like a heel pretending I did. There was something I liked about this man, Charlie Kuntz, and I hated lying to him.

"Well now, young fella, what did you want to talk to me about?"

He leaned back in his chair, locking his fingers behind his head.

"Like to talk to you about a story I'm working on for the Detroit News and I have a feeling that you know Chicago and the people in it like the back of your hand."

"That I do, my boy. That I do. What's your story about?"

"I want to do a human-interest piece on the late Alden Whitaker. How he started out, how he came to connect with Henry Ford…you know, tie it to Detroit for our readers. I want to go on to tell how his daughter is managing the business without him. I thought you could tell me if her husband is involved in any way with the company. That kind of thing."

He squinted with his eyes and nodded. "Well, first of all," he began, "you don't do your homework very well." He brought his arms forward and leaned on his desk. "Phyllis doesn't manage the business. In fact, she has nothing to do with running any *part* of the business. That's all taken care of by his right hand man in the company at the time of his death. His will stipulated how the profits were to be handled: where the money would go. Most of it is poured right back into *Whitaker Tire*. He specified...oh, I don't know, maybe four or five charities that the company would donate to annually. And as far as Phyllis, well she gets a bit of a monthly income, too. Not sure how much, but I'd heard it wasn't all that great, compared to what the company is earning; especially now since they're supplying the war effort."

"He left her *nothing*?" I was astounded.

"Oh, now don't be an idiot, boy! Of *course* he left her *something*. She got the estate free and clear; a huge place with lots of acreage and two guesthouses at the rear of the property. I think one serves as the maid's quarters and then she's got that bodyguard and driver, and a second driver who is also her personal mechanic. They live in the other guesthouse. He left her a couple of pretty fine cars, and then there was the bank account totaling almost five million in cash. I wouldn't call that *nothing*."

He picked up the bottle of bourbon and topped off my glass and then his own.

55

He continued, "Personally, Alden Whitaker was one
S.O.B. Shrewd as hell and ruder than necessary to most
people. I betcha Ruth Whitaker could attest to that, if the
story is to be believed. Seems Alden had a wife named
Ruth, who is Phyllis's mother, before he came to
Chicago. They say she ended up hating him, and run off.
It's told that Phyllis was only four or five years old when
her mother run off and never looked back. But I hear tell
that him and Ford got along just peachy. Both had the
same temperament, both had the same drive, and both
had the same outlook on things...Hitler, being one. They
both admired the dirty rotten so and so. I guess Ford *still*
admires that damn Nazi."

"Well, what about this daughter, Phyllis? If she has
no part in running the business, what takes up her time
nowadays? How's she doing without her father around?"

"I hope you're planning on speaking to her because
she could answer you better than I can. What I know is
just hearsay and my own opinion."

I told him that I was planning on doing just that, but I
hadn't been able to connect with her yet to set up a time
for the interview; but I assured him that she *had* agreed to
one. There I was, lying to him again. I usually had no
problem stretching the truth when working on a case. If it
brought the needed results, so what? What did I care? But
somehow, with Charlie Kuntz, I cared. There was a part
of me that hated myself for sitting in his chair, drinking
his bourbon and lying to him.

He went on to tell me that following her father's
death, she'd sort of gone wild; spending money like it
was water. Many thought she was trying to fill a void. He

told me of the people she would hire and fire at the drop of a hat, the designers she'd hired to create new wardrobes, the hobby she'd picked up of playing the thoroughbreds at the track. He told me of the travels to Europe and South America and the nearly dozen men she went through in the space of a year and a half.

"But I have my own theory." He rubbed the white whiskers protruding from his chin. He was overdue for a shave. "I don't think it was to fill a void, like most think. I believe it was out of spite."

"Out of *spite*?" I asked.

"Yep. Old Whitaker wielded a heavy hand; laid down the law. He wouldn't let her live her own life. He ruined the one relationship that made her happy. You know about Calvert?"

I nodded that I did.

"Well, whatever Jack Calvert was or wasn't, she loved him with all her heart. You could tell that just by seeing the way she looked at him. But, once again, old man Whitaker knew best. Oh, I don't figure Calvert was too broken up about the separation, but she sure was. I'm sure Alden offered to pay him off and that made Calvert agreeable.

Talk was that he married her for money anyway, even though she would've never believed that." He started to laugh. He smacked the desk with his open palm and pointed at me with his forefinger. "And ya wanna hear a good one?"

I nodded.

"It's the damndest thing, but Calvert is a staunch Catholic. Won't break any of their rules. He wouldn't miss a mass if his life depended on it. But outside the Church, he was some type of collector for Chicago's own, Capone. Hands dirty as hell, but he thinks as long as he follows the rules of the Church, he's got a reserved spot in Heaven. Anyway, he moved on some years ago. I think New York City…ah, maybe it was Boston. Who knows? Out on the east coast somewhere. Month or two ago I heard a rumor he was back here, but I haven't heard anything more on that one."

I shook my head then swallowed the last of my bourbon. "Well, what about this one she's with now? You think he married her for money, also?" I was eager to hear what he would say in sizing up the husband who was going out on her. I listened intently.

"Eddie? Seems to be a fine young man, but I guess I never understood it. It's the strangest thing. Kid could be her son. I mean, she's more than twenty years older than him. She's not a bad looking woman, but have you seen *him*? He's one handsome guy.

He's got looks most men would want. And I'm sure he could have any young dame that looked at him twice. And, believe me; most of them *do* look *more* than twice."

He paused and picked up the dead cigar that was sitting in a green glass ashtray on his desk. Putting it between his teeth, he lit it, and took a long, slow pull on it. He picked up the bourbon again, reaching it out toward me, but I covered my glass with the palm of my hand and shook my head. He pulled the bottle back and poured more into his own glass, filling it almost to the brim.

"What? You think he might just play around on the side then?"

He turned his head to the left and stared out the window portion of the door to the working area of the Trib, watching as the reporters pecked away at their typewriters. I knew he was carefully contemplating the question and trying to formulate his words to explain his view of the situation. I let him consider it in silence and waited for his answer. Finally, he turned back and took a sip of his drink. He looked at me. "Well, if my instincts are anything to go by, I would have to say no. I've never seen him with anyone else and there's never been any talk of it. Now there might be some who think he's not sincere about her, or that he might have wandering eyes, 'cause word got out that he took out a hefty insurance policy on her. But last I knew, that's not a crime and it's not proof of infidelity. I still say he truly loves her. I believe that." He puffed on his cigar again and then waved it in the air. "Ah, but what the hell do I know? I could have it all wrong. Here's what I *do* know about Eddie Killburn, though."

He proceeded to tell me that Eddie Killburn was in England when the war broke out in Europe in the beginning of September, 1939, and felt the pull to offer his services. The young man joined their Royal Air Force, using his previous flight experience to maneuver their spitfires. Six months into it, his spitfire stalled as he was climbing. That ended his military career as he knew it—he'd permanently injured his left leg. Nothing to put him in a wheel chair, but that was it for him, nonetheless. After some months of recuperating in a hospital in

Nottingham, England, Eddie returned home to the U.S. Instead of settling down once again in his native New York, he showed up in Chicago to start anew. He'd met Phyllis and married her after a brief, whirlwind courtship. Eddie Killburn now played piano and sang at the *Easy Street Lounge* and was very good at it. He also did local volunteer work for the United States military.

The door opened to the office and a young reporter barged in.

"Sorry Chief, but all hell is busting loose over at the 12th District Courthouse. The verdict is in in the Fredo Mancuso case!"

Charlie Kuntz jump up from his chair. Waving his cigar, he yelled, "Well, get your butt down there! What's the matter with you?"

The reporter left the office in a hurry, slamming the door, leaving us alone again. The editor returned to his seat and ran his hand through his hair.

"The dummy!" he said of the young reporter. "I guess I forgot I have a paper to run."

"I guess I forgot you do, too," I said, rising from the chair. I extended my hand to shake his. "You've been a great help. I've got an angle on this one already. Thanks for everything. I better let you get back to work."

I turned to leave.

"Hey, Flanagan." I turned back to him with my hand on the doorknob. "I'd like to be able to say send me a copy of that story when you write it, but we both know there won't be any story."

I just stared at him and felt the inner heat yet again.

"But no matter," he continued." I enjoyed this. Come back and talk any time. But just so you know, last time I saw Ty Carver was about seven months ago, I'd say. He had excellent vision…in *both* eyes."

He took another puff of the cigar and exhaled toward the ceiling. I smiled sheepishly. He had me. It was no surprise to me that I hadn't fooled him. Charlie Kuntz knew way too much about human nature. He was an expert. I thanked him again and let myself out of his office.

Judith White

CHAPTER EIGHT

Before grabbing my hat and coat from Harry's cubicle, I picked up the receiver of his phone and dialed his house. No one answered after eight rings, so it was safe to assume Myra was still at her mothers. I wasn't quite sure what to do with myself, but I couldn't stay inside the offices of the Chicago Tribune.

Stepping outside was like stepping into an arctic blast. As cold as it was, the wind felt good on my face; but it wouldn't feel good for long. The Windy City was living up to its name. I looked to the left on W. Washington Blvd. I looked to the right. Nothing caught my attention. Where was I going to go? What was I going to do? I looked straight across the street and saw a moving picture theater. The marquee above The Bijou said '*Junior G-Men of the Air*' starring Lionel Atwill and '*The Dead End Kids*'. I had actually seen this movie last spring, when it first came out; Gran had asked me to take her to see it. She loved *The Dead End Kids*, and I enjoyed them, too. Lionel Atwill; well, I could take him or leave him. It was another wartime movie like so many others coming out of Hollywood since we'd been attacked at Pearl Harbor and had entered the fight.

I carefully crossed the street, which was slick with dirty slush. The sky was darkening. It appeared that another dose of snow would blanket the city before long. Near the ticket window was a sign that told me the next showing was at 4:15. I looked at my watch. It was 3:58 at the moment. Three teenage girls stood between the ticket window and me. They whispered in each other's ears and giggled. The dame behind the glass had her back to us and it looked like she was counting money from the register, but she was taking her good old time and I felt a bit irritated at that. I didn't know if it was from the bourbon or the conflicting information Charlie Kuntz had given me, but my headache was worse, and because of that, my patience was wearing thin. Then she turned around. My mood softened at the sight of her. With her delicate facial features and long blond hair parted on the side, she looked like Veronica Lake, one of my all-time favorites.

"Hello girls. Three tickets?" she asked, smiling.

They nodded their heads and continued their giggling. She ripped off the tickets from the roll and took their change. I approached the window with what I thought might be my most charming smile.

"Hello, there! One, please."

She slid my ticket underneath the glass partition and took my twenty-five cents without as much as a glance in my direction. Ah well, so much for trying to be flirtatious.

I entered the lobby of the theater, stamping the slush from my shoes just inside the doorway. Once inside and seated, I counted no more than twenty viewers, including myself and the girls. The show started off with two newsreels. The first was a British production making a mockery of the German troops and the theater filled with laughter: a bit of a break from the seriousness of the situation. The second was titled *Hitler Marches on Europe*. I found them both to be interesting, but when the film started, I pulled my mind away to consider what I'd learned back at the Trib. I'd spent nearly two hours talking to Charlie Kuntz and it seemed everything he'd told me about Eddie Killburn was conflicting to the story Phyllis had laid out. Of course, Phyllis lived with the man and Charlie didn't. Yet, I couldn't discount his news hound instinct. And what was that about volunteering for the military? You aren't secretive about what you're doing when all you're doing is volunteer work. Phyllis was definitely leery of what his position was and was obviously frightened. Maybe he invented the volunteer angle for the general public in Chicago. What could he possibly be doing to throw them off the track? Selling war bonds? Conducting black out raids? Scanning the skies for enemy aircraft? Even though the military angle had me worried and curious, I was hired to find out who he was seeing, if he *was* seeing anyone. Both Harry and Charlie had heard no rumors and had not seen him with any other woman. Could Phyllis just be paranoid? That wouldn't be all that farfetched, given the age difference. Either Phyllis was insecure and overreacting, or her husband was pulling a fast one on all of us.

I slid down in my seat, laying my head against the back of it. I needed to close my eyes for a moment. In the darkness, I could hear the girls whispering up nearer the big screen. Someone from across the theater let out a loud "*Sh!*" aimed in their direction—they snickered in response. From the screen I could hear the voice of Hunts Hall say they couldn't trust the police with the information; they had to deal with the spies themselves. That's the last thing I remembered. The next thing I knew, someone was gently nudging my shoulder.

"Hey, Mister. Come on, Mister, wake up. The movie's over."

I opened my eyes to see 'Veronica Lake's' face just inches from mine. I smiled and then looked around to find a theater full of empty seats. I straightened in the chair and cleared my throat.

"Oh, sorry. I guess I dozed."

"You sure did!" she said with disgust in her voice.

She turned on her heel and marched up the aisle and disappeared from sight. I stayed in my seat maybe a minute more, not longer, trying to clear the cobwebs from my head. Once in the lobby, I asked her, "Hey, sister. You wouldn't happen to know where the *Easy Street Lounge* is, would you? If so, how do I get there from here?"

"Head that way," she said, pointing. "Turn right at the fourth intersection onto Michigan Avenue. It'll be three blocks down on your right."

I thanked her and started for the door, but her voice made me turn to her again.

"I got a brother and you ain't him, so I *ain't* your sister!"

She had a point.

****

I retrieved the Ford from the lot across the street and followed her directions. After my little catnap, my headache was gone and I was hungry. I thought it was time to check out Eddie Killburn, and what better place than the *Easy Street Lounge*? As soon as I pulled into the lot reserved for parking at the lounge, snowflakes the size of nickels started falling from the sky. If Detroit wasn't getting snow tonight, they surely would be tomorrow. As I locked the auto and pocketed the key, my thoughts turned to my grandmother. I hoped she was alright. I'd only been gone a day, but she was eighty-two, for God's sake. I'd have to give her a call, maybe tomorrow.

The lounge was dimly lit. The carpet was an olive green, the same color as the padded circular booths that lined the walls. The tables in the middle of the room were clothed with the same green in a green and ivory print; four heavy mahogany chairs were placed at each. A large gold ashtray sat in the middle of each table, along with a lit ivory colored candle. A long polished mahogany bar lined three quarters of one wall and a baby grand piano sat to its left. The atmosphere in the *Easy Street Lounge* was one of upper class, but with warmth, not haughtiness.

I glanced at my watch. It was 6:52. It wasn't crowded and probably wouldn't be tonight because of the nastiness of the conditions outside: and it was Thursday. I could well imagine the lounge to be jam packed most

Fridays and Saturdays. I chose one of the booths and sat down. They were high backed, providing maximum privacy from the occupants on either side. It hadn't been two minutes when I was approached by a woman appearing to be no more than twenty-six or twenty-seven years old. She wore an ivory short-sleeved blouse and a pair of olive green shorts that came just above mid-thigh. Her light brown hair was worn in one of the new short and wavy styles. The young woman had a pleasant face and a pretty smile. On a small round tray, she poised her pen over an order pad.

"Hello, I'm Ginny. Welcome to Easy Street. What can I get you?"

That was cute. W*elcome to Easy Street*. Didn't I wish?

"What have you got?" I inquired.

"Our special tonight is roasted chicken. We also have porterhouse steak, pot ro—"

I cut her off. "I'll have that….the steak. Medium. Just bring whatever it comes with. I'll take black coffee with that."

She walked away without a word. I pulled out my Lucky Strikes from my suit coat pocket and lit one. I inhaled deeply and looked around at the other occupants. There was a young couple sitting at a table, and the woman kept holding up her left hand and admiring the ring she wore on it. *Newly engaged*, I thought. A middle-aged man sat alone at a table, eating the roasted chicken special with a frosty mug of beer, half empty. His brief case was on the chair next to him. *In town on business*, I thought. Three gentlemen in suits were perched at the bar with drinks in front of them. They all sat at least one stool apart, which meant they weren't there together. *Unwinding before heading home from work*, I thought. I couldn't tell who was in the booth to my left or right, but undoubtedly there was someone to my right because Ginny had just served a drink to the table and then continued on to me to give me my coffee. I took a sip and then puffed on my cigarette.

The door opened and I felt a rush of cold air. I turned to see two middle-aged couples enter and brush the snow from their outer clothing. The men removed their hats and looked around for a place to sit. All four were laughing about something as they made their way to a booth in the far corner, directly across from the piano that sat empty, so far. I didn't know whether Eddie Killburn would be entertaining tonight; if not, I'd still get a meal out of my trip to the lounge.

I didn't wait long for my dinner. The plate Ginny sat before me contained the steak, mashed potatoes and brown gravy, tomato slices, corn and warm, freshly baked bread. The meat was tender and the coffee was the best I'd ever tasted. I was so intent on eating that it startled me when the piano keys sounded. It was 7:35. I looked up and there he was, Eddie Killburn. He began to speak while brushing the keys softly.

"Welcome to Easy Street." *That must be a catch phrase here*, I thought. "I see some beautiful faces here tonight. Have you seen the weather? Brrr." He shivered as if he were cold. "I bet I know what you're thinking," he said, flashing a winning smile and displaying perfect white teeth and the dimple in his cheek. "You're thinking of April." Then he began to play and sing *I'll Remember April*, the Woody Herman hit of the previous year. I sat back, pushing my plate away and moving my coffee cup closer, and lit another cigarette. Charlie Kuntz was right; Eddie was good…he was *really* good. His voice was deep and melodic. I absorbed the sounds and soaked in the relaxing atmosphere. He followed with *I've Got a Gal in Kalamazoo* by Glenn Miller and played Benny Goodman's instrumental, *Jersey Bounce,* before taking a brief break.

Ginny was heading my way with the coffee pot when she made a detour to the piano as Eddie stood.

"Get you something, Eddie?"

"Not right now, but thanks. I think I'll just go out back and stretch this bum leg."

I saw something in her eyes when she looked at him. I tried to capture his expression, but I was too late. He was on the move, dragging his rigid left leg behind him as he headed toward the rear of the lounge. Her eyes never left his back until he was out of sight. It was only then that she continued in my direction, refilling my cup when she arrived.

"Your boyfriend?" I casually asked.

"Who? Eddie?" She laughed softly. "Nah, he's just a good friend."

She sat down on the edge of my booth and took out her order pad. She ripped off the top sheet and started to add up my bill.

I pressed further. "You two would look good together. I could've sworn you were an item."

She looked up and her eyes traveled in the direction that Eddie had made his departure.

"It might've happened at one time, but Eddie met someone right here in the lounge, and that was that." She sighed. "All the good ones are taken."

She finished her addition and pushed the bill over to me. Ginny rose and walked away from the table. Five minutes later, Eddie was back at the keys for a second set. I stayed, listening to four more songs. I was about to leave when he seemed to be coming my way. I froze. I didn't want him to be aware of me, so I hunkered down in my seat and was relieved when he deposited himself in the booth to my right, where Ginny had served the drink earlier. I slid around to the other side of the booth, getting closer to where he now sat. I heard him talking to someone.

"Hi, Lou. How you doing tonight?"

"Wonderful, as always." The voice was a bit deep and husky, but feminine and sensual.

Eddie called out to the bartender, "Turk, how about a vodka martini? Three olives." He must've turned to Lou then. "Want another, Lou?" Lou either nodded or shook her head, because I didn't hear a response. "Just the martini, Turk. Thanks."

Eddie resumed his conversation with Lou. "Well, how's the sound tonight? How am I doing?"

"You're brilliant. You're absolutely brilliant, as always. Why else would I spend my evenings listening to you? You're a genius."

This was getting good. Finally a sign of his infidelity—maybe poster boy wasn't so innocent after all.

I barely breathed, straining to hear all that was being said.

Eddie chuckled. "Lou, you are always so good for my ego. You know that?"

"Uh huh. And I could be a lot better for it if someone wasn't in the way. What, no one with you tonight?"

"No, she's into a good book and didn't want to leave it," Eddie answered.

"Oh phooey!" Lou said. "She's always either reading a book or she has a headache or she's tired. She doesn't seem to be as big a fan as I am."

"Now, now. Be nice." Eddie chuckled again.

"Darling, that *is* being nice! But I'll show you how *really* nice I can be when I get back from the little boy's room. Now don't you move, Eddie Killburn!"

I stiffened and jerked away from having my ear stuck to the back of the booth. Little boy's room? What the hell? I watched as Lou rose from the seat. Wearing an expensive black suit, white shirt opened at the collar and a silky white scarf draped around his neck, he headed for the men's room. He was slightly built, maybe about five feet seven inches tall, with slicked back black hair and a pencil thin mustache on an otherwise clean shaven face. On each of his fingers he wore a ring. Lou was a man, and he had a swivel in his hips that would rival that of any classy broad. I was so intent on checking him out that I didn't hear Ginny approach Eddie at the booth behind me.

"Why do you sit with him? He's disgusting!" she said.

"Oh, Lou's alright. He's harmless. Just a bit of a leap," Eddie said. "He's a fan of my music, and I can't chase my fans away."

"I still say he's disgusting."

I heard Eddie thank her for the drink and she walked away.

I picked up my tab and mentally added it, just to make sure Ginny had made no mistake on her calculation. I pulled out a five-dollar bill and laid it alongside the check, smiling inwardly at the thought of her face when she saw what a hefty tip I'd left her.

Outside the snow had been piling up. As I started the Model A, I couldn't help but laugh at the thought of Phyllis's reaction if I had to tell her that her husband was seeing another man. I left the auto running as I cleared the windows and headlights. I was looking forward to climbing into bed back at the house. Today had been a very long day.

Judith White

CHAPTER NINE

The morning brought blinding sunlight streaming through the spare bedroom's only window. I squinted at the clock. It was just after eight. The aroma of coffee entered my nostrils. Someone was up and moving around in the kitchen and I was willing to bet that someone was Myra.

When I'd arrived back at the house last night, I had found the door unlocked. It was quiet and one of the living room table lamps was ablaze. They'd obviously turned in for the night. A note was propped up against the base of the lamp, written in Myra's hand, and it told me that the spare room was ready to occupy. The bed was warm and comfortable and I had no trouble falling asleep. If a train passed during the night, I sure didn't hear it.

I dressed and headed for the kitchen. I found Myra whipping some sort of batter and humming a tune softly. She wore a dark blue robe and her belly was protruding, separating the front opening, exposing a lighter blue nightgown. Her hair, pulled back in a loose bun, was damp. Apparently, she'd already showered for the day.

"Someone is in a good mood, huh?" I asked as I entered the kitchen.

She jumped. "Oh Mr. Flanagan, you startled me." She started to laugh softly.

"Oh, didn't mean to do that. And when are you going to start calling me Sam?"

She blushed. "Sit down. I'll pour you some coffee. I hope you like hot cakes."

I did as I was told and sipped at the coffee as I watched her pour the batter onto the hot griddle.

"Can I help with anything?" I offered.

"If you want to help, you can get the orange juice out."

Again, I did what I was told. She continued her humming as she flipped the cakes. I heard the front door open and close and Harry came in with the morning edition of the Tribune. He got himself a cup of coffee and sat at the table across from me, muttering a 'good morning' while browsing the front page. I saw the day's headline:

President Roosevelt and British Prime Minister Winston Churchill open a wartime conference in Casablanca.

It was the first time an American President had traveled overseas in an airplane.

As Harry continued looking at the newspaper, he said, "I'm not going into the Trib until much later today.

Some of the guys get together every once in a while and have an afternoon poker game. Wanna go, Sam?" And then, looking over the paper at me, he added, "Or did you have something in mind for me today as far as the Killburn case?"

I was about to answer him when a loud bang came from Myra's direction. We both jumped and looked just in time to see the spatula bounce off the edge of the stove and hit the tiled floor. Neither of us spoke.

Myra turned to face Harry with her hands on her hips and yelled, "What *day* is it?"

Shocked by her outburst, Harry responded, "Uh...it's Friday."

"And what is the *date*?"

"Uh...it's the fourteenth."

"And just what *is* January fourteenth?"

Myra was trying to control her anger, but it wasn't working. Harry turned to me in a silent plea for help, but I just shrugged. I had a hunch that we wouldn't have to wait long for Myra to tell us just what the date meant. I was right.

"*I was born thirty-one years ago today, Harry! I shouldn't have to remind you of that!*" she screamed.

She paused, took a deep breath, and continued in a much more controlled voice. "Now, I want a new dress, and I am not gonna make it. I want a store bought one. You're takin' me shoppin'. I want to go to *Woolworth* and you can buy me dinner there, too. But first, you're takin' me to Moms for a visit." She turned in my direction, "You'll meet us for dinner, Sam."

With that, she turned on her heel and marched into their bedroom, slamming the door. We heard it open again almost immediately and she yelled, *"And get your own damn hot cakes!"*

We heard the door slam again.

Harry turned to me, looking stunned. "What on earth has gotten into that woman?"

I laughed out loud. "I'd say a whole lot of sense."

****

Harry and a much happier Myra left the house about 10:30 with my promise that I would meet them at *Woolworth* about 4:30. At Harry's desk, I took a sheet of paper and picked up one of his pencils. Heading toward the kitchen, I wanted to write down what I knew about this case. I poured myself another cup of coffee and sat at the table. But then I thought about my grandmother. I wanted to call her and see if all was okay, but I'd forgotten to mention it to Harry. I didn't want to take liberties when they'd been so kind in giving me a place to stay. I was sure he wouldn't mind, as long as I paid for the call. Reaching in my pocket, I pulled out a dollar bill and set it near the sink. I had no idea how much it would cost, but I thought the dollar would more than cover it. I dialed the number and Gran answered after the third ring.

"Hello? Who is this, please?" she asked, loudly.

"Hi, Gran. It's me, Sam. Everything alright on the home front?"

"What?" she yelled. "*Who?*"

"*Sam!*" I yelled back.

"Oh, he ain't here. He's out of the country, doin' detective work. Call another day."

"No, Gran. It's—"

But she'd hung up. I frowned; *out of the country? I shook my head*, put the phone back in its cradle, and picked it right back up again. Midway through redialing the house, I stopped. *Let's analyze this situation*, I thought to myself. *If I call back, she might not answer, thinking I'm the one who is still looking for Sam. If she does answer, she might still think I'm that someone else looking for Sam, and I'll have two long distanced calls to pay for.* She had answered the phone and that meant she was alright…that was good enough for me.

On paper, I briefly outlined my conversation with Phyllis Killburn at my office two days ago. Was it really only two days ago that she'd entered my office and I had taken on this case? It seemed much longer ago than that. I made notes on my conversation with the hardware store owner. I wrote down the highlights of my conversation with Charlie Kuntz and summarized my evening at the *Easy Street Lounge*. I was reading and rereading what I'd written down. The one thing that kept surfacing in my mind was that Eddie Killburn didn't seem to be the type to be hiding a dame on the side; he seemed too damned *nice*. That was it; he was *nice*. Everyone I talked to gave me the impression that he was a straight arrow; a good guy. Everyone I'd talked to so far—Charlie Kuntz, Ginny, the waitress at the *Easy Street Lounge*, and even Harry—seemed to like him. And then there was Lou. Could Eddie not only be going out on his wife, but could he be doing that with another man? Deep in my gut I didn't think that was the situation. From the conversation I had heard last night, it seemed that it was Lou who was taken with Eddie, but not the other way around. Even though I didn't really know Eddie, I didn't think he swung that way. I could be wrong, but I doubted it.

Another thing that bothered me was this undercover work he was allegedly involved in: secret missions, spying for the country. But *which* country? Again, he didn't seem the type. But what *was* the type? If he *were* involved in espionage, then he was perfect for it because he *didn't seem the type*. In this business, I'd learned long ago not to go on appearances because things were rarely what they seemed.

I was still mulling these things over when there came a knock on the front door. I thought about just staying where I was and not answering. After all, this was Harry and Myra's place and they weren't home. I decided against that course of action when a loud second knocking sounded. It was more like three heavy pounds. *BOOM, BOOM, BOOM.* I made my way to the front of the house, noticing through the window a 1942 black Ford Super Deluxe parked across the street. Hmm, that was interesting. I opened the door to find the fat guy I had seen on the bus from Detroit. He was the guy I'd seen with Phyllis coming out of *Violet Hour*.

"Da Mrs. wants ta see ya," he stated in a monotone.

"Okay, tell her I'll give her a call and be around in the next couple of days."

I started to shut the door when he blocked it with a huge hand and stuck his foot between it and the jamb.

"Hey—!" I started to protest, but he shoved his way into the house and stood in the small entryway.

"Da Mrs. wants ta see ya. She wants dat I should bring ya wid me now."

Man, this big boy was a real genius. I could tell that by his speech.

"Can I at least grab my coat?"

He didn't respond, but he didn't try to stop me from moving into the spare bedroom, either, nor did he follow me. He waited like a gentleman, right where he was. Retrieving my coat from the foot of the bed, I suddenly had a thought. I wasn't going anywhere with this big lug unprepared. The Luger I'd bought a couple of days ago was in my overnight bag, which was under the bed. I stooped to get it, making sure it was loaded, and then slipped it into the side pocket of my overcoat.

"Alright, take me to your leader," I cracked to him as we headed out.

The inside of the Super Deluxe was cleaner than clean—not a speck of dirt or dust anywhere. It was comfortable and roomy and still smelled new. *Boy, what I wouldn't give*, I thought.

I turned to him, "So what's your name?"

I waited for an answer, but none came. He kept his eyes straight ahead.

"Okay, so why don't you tell me what the Mrs. wants to see me about?"

Still, he was unresponsive.

"She's not taking me off the case, is she?"

Now I was getting mad. I'd asked him three questions to which he didn't even grunt in reply. I decided to get smart with him.

"So, bud, whatcha been doin' the last couple of days? I bet you bathed somewhere in all that time."

I noticed there was no unpleasant odor making its way toward me—nothing. This was the type of goon who took orders and did only what he was told. He was told to fetch me and bring me to his boss, and that's what he was doing; nothing more. I decided to give it a rest and turned to view the scenery on the drive to the Whitaker estate. I figured Phyllis probably stayed in the house that Daddy built and just moved her boy in; no sense in giving up a good thing. How long her boy would be residing there was the question.

****

We followed a circular drive and parked at the front entrance. The house was a red-bricked structure with three floors to it. Black shutters hung at each window. The walkway and porch had been cleared of any snow, but it hung on the pine trees gracing the yard. I looked at the massive front lawn, now deeply buried under a few inches of the white powder. Three white marble birdbaths stood in the middle, vacant of their intended occupants, but filled with the flakes.

Harry's whole house could've fit into the living area I was directed to. I made my way to the sofa and sat down to wait for Mrs. Killburn, using the time to take in my surroundings. The carpet was green, gold and pink floral. The sofas, both of them, were white and sat perpendicular to each other. A glass coffee table sat in front of them, and was positioned in front of a huge marble fireplace. On the table a bouquet of various flowers emerged from a tall, slender crystal vase. A crystal ashtray and cigarette lighter sat closer to the edge, nearer the sofas.

At one end of the room a grand piano sat with a gigantic bust of some Roman god, I figured, behind it on a pedestal. Across from the piano was another seating area; two white chairs with an ottoman in front of one and a glass end table with a crystal lamp on it in between. The walls were white and the curtains, which spanned the whole wall behind the piano, were the same floral pattern as the carpeting. The wall directly opposite the window was taken up completely with bookshelves. A ladder that slid along the shelves sat in the corner. Out from the bookshelves sat a very heavy looking mahogany desk with nothing on it but a green desk lamp and a penholder containing a few writing instruments. *What in the world would it be like*? I thought to myself.

I glanced at my watch. It was 11:47. I'd already been here a little over ten minutes with no sign of Phyllis. I leaned forward with my elbows on my knees as I continued to look around. On the wall above the fireplace was a monstrous portrait of a man. It showed the whole of him standing and looking off to his right, a dour look on his face. He was tall and lanky, balding, with round black framed glasses. This had to be Alden Whitaker, judging by the old news clipping I'd seen of the engagement announcement.

The house appeared quiet. I was wondering if Phyllis Killburn was going to show up or if she'd even remembered that she'd sent her boy to get me. I wasn't long on patience, never had been. I looked at my watch again. It was 12:04. I'd give the lady of the house just five more minutes. If she didn't show by then, I was getting out of here. I'd walk back to Harry's if I had to. No amount of money in the world could make me this woman's lap dog.

CHAPTER TEN

Phyllis Killburn must've read my mind, because just as I was about to get up and leave the premises, she walked in with the back of her hand touching her forehead.

"Oh, Mr. Flanagan, I have such a grueling headache. I was lying down for a bit."

I didn't like *that* one bit. Her lying down while I was sitting here, waiting to see her at *her* bequest? No, I didn't like it at all, but I kept quiet and said nothing.

I noticed that when she walked into the room she was followed by the fat man. He stood in the doorway of the room playing the role of protector; acting as guard dog.

She turned to him and, with a wave of her hand, said "That's fine, Augie, I'll be alright."

He didn't look convinced, and turned his gaze toward me.

"Go on, Augie!" she said a bit more forcefully. "I'll call you if I need you."

He left us.

She was dressed in some type of silky lounging outfit. She wore jade colored slacks that stopped at the top of her ankles, with a matching long sleeved silk top that hung down to right above her knees. She wore jade pumps with a row of white feathery looking material at the top of her foot. *The luxurious slippers of the wealthy*, I thought.

"Now, Mr. Flanagan, I know you've been in town and I want to hear how you're progressing. Have you found out anything? Seen him with anyone? I assume you've been working on the case."

I wondered how she knew I'd been in town, but I didn't ask her. Before I could answer her, a maid came in with a glass of red wine on a silver tray and set it on the table in front of Phyllis.

"Brigitte, bring Mr. Flanagan something." She pronounced it bree-SHEET. Phyllis turned to me as the maid waited. "Wine? Coffee? Something stronger? I never touch the hard liquor, myself. Can't stand any of it. It's like poison to me, but we have anything you could want."

I told her I'd take a little scotch on the rocks, if she didn't mind. My eyes followed the maid as she left. She was stunning! Tall and slender, her face appeared to be angelic and seductive all at once. Her full lips were tinted pink and her long black lashes framed very blue eyes. Her blond hair was worn pulled back in some sort of tie at the nape of her neck and bangs hung across her forehead.

"Before I get into this, there's been something I've been wondering. Why me? Why come all the way to

Detroit to hire a private dick? Why not find one right here in town?"

"Mr. Flanagan, Chicago *knows* me; the people know every little thing I do. I was hoping this wouldn't get out until it had to. *If* it has to." She shrugged. "I guess that's why."

I rubbed at the stubble on my chin. It made sense. I started to tell her what I'd been doing when Brigitte came back in with my drink on the little silver tray.

"Will zat be all, Madam?" Brigitte asked, with an attractive French accent.

Phyllis sipped at her wine, waving her hand, indicating Brigitte could take her leave. I waited until she was gone.

"What about her?" I nodded toward the doorway that Brigitte had just passed through.

"What about her...what?"

"Well, do you think Mr. Killburn could be fooling around with the maid?" I asked.

She let out a laugh as if I'd just told her a joke. She was amused.

"With *Brigitte*?" she laughed again. "Absolutely not!"

"Why not? She's young. She's very attractive."

"And she's very loyal, Mr. Flanagan. She's very, very loyal to me! She has nothing to do with any of this. Besides, she corresponds with a Philippe back in Quebec. I assume there is something a little more than just friendship between them."

Her tone of voice cautioned me not to pursue it, so I didn't. I skipped my discussion with Charlie Kuntz, but told her about my visit to the *Easy Street Lounge* and what I had observed, which, in my opinion, was nothing of consequence. She took a sip of wine and extracted a cigarette from a gold case. I lit it for her with her crystal lighter. She took a drag, blew the smoke toward the ceiling, and then turned to me with an amused look on her face.

"And I suppose you came across *Ginny* there?" She mentioned the name with distaste. "She's nothing but a tart. She had a thing for Eddie when I first met him, and I suspect still has a thing for him. But he wouldn't give her a second look. She's not involved, either."

My assessment of Ginny and her assessment of Ginny were two different things, but I let that slide. I wondered if she even knew what a real tart was. Ginny didn't appear to be a tart, in my opinion. I suspected jealousy was fueling Phyllis when it came to the waitress.

"Well, do you have any other ideas? 'Cause I gotta tell you, everything I've seen points to he isn't seeing anyone...so far, that is. It's early days. Unless you think Lou has anything to do with this."

My mind traveled back to the booth next to mine at the lounge and Eddie's conversation with the man who liked his music.

She laughed again. "*That* fruitcake? No, no, Eddie's not into *that*, Mr. Flanagan, I can assure you."

She looked down at her hands, adjusting her wedding ring. She got very quiet and contemplative.

"I'm scared, Mr. Flanagan. I'm really very scared," she said softly. Then she startled me by whispering, "I think he's going to try to kill me."

She told me of an argument that occurred the night she'd contacted me in Detroit.

Eddie had come home from the lounge drunk. He'd actually come home about 4:00 a.m. the next morning, and she couldn't be sure he hadn't stopped off somewhere in between. She'd never asked because she didn't want to know at the time. He'd started a loud argument and told her he didn't want to be with her anymore, and it was just a matter of time. She told me she'd gathered up the courage to confront him with her suspicions of his seeing someone else and he'd just laughed in her face, saying she might not be around to find out.

"Is that why you bought the Luger?" I asked.

She looked startled. "You *know* about that?" I said nothing and she went on, "Yes. I somehow thought I might need it for protection. This isn't the first time he's threatened me."

****

I was back in the Super Deluxe with Augie at the wheel. Having a conversation with the guy wasn't an option, so I just took in the sights of the city from the passenger seat. I spotted a sign atop a business a couple of blocks up ahead and leaned forward, pointing through the windshield.

"There," I said. "Pull over at *Mama Tortelli's Bakery.*"

He looked at me with doubt in his eyes. I leaned back in my seat once again and shrugged.

"Okay, fine by me. But how you gonna explain to the Mrs. why you wouldn't let me do the job she's paying me for?"

When we reached the bakery, he pulled up to the curb right in front. He stayed in the car and kept it running while I entered the building. The interior was warm with the aroma of apples and cinnamon igniting my senses. A display case held pastries that looked heavenly. I felt emptiness in my stomach; I was getting hungry. A woman in her seventies stood behind the counter, waiting for me to state what I wanted. I had assumed this was Mama Tortelli.

"Got any cakes already baked?" I asked.

"I gotta two. You wanna da chocolate, or da coconut?"

I told her the chocolate would do and asked if she could write 'Happy Birthday, Myra' on it. As she held the tube of icing above the cake, I turned back to all the baked goods. There were dozens of cookies on a tray inside the case. I was a sucker for cookies, especially peanut butter. As I was bent over, eying them, she asked me something in her thick Italian accent…she asked if Myra was a little woman. I straightened and faced her, wondering what in the world that had to do with anything.

"Uh, yeah. As a matter of fact, she is. Hey, throw in a couple of these peanut butter cookies, too, alright?"

She nodded and continued writing the birthday greeting. When she was done, she boxed the cake and loosely wrapped the cookies in tissue paper. I paid her and left. I returned to the car, carefully placing the box on my lap, and handed Augie a cookie. He hesitated before taking it and eyed the packaged cake.

"Hey, I figured since I was in there..."

He pulled away from the curb and we ate our cookies in silence. He had me back at Harry's within five minutes. I immediately went to the kitchen. Before showering for my appointment with Harry and Myra at *Woolworth*, I wanted to surprise Myra by setting the cake out on the table along with a flower I'd pinched from Phyllis's table top bouquet.

I hunted in the cupboards for a vase and, not finding one, I filled a drinking glass with water, inserting the yellow rose. I gently lifted the cake from the box and set it next to the makeshift vase. Oh boy! Myra was going to be surprised, alright. In Mama Tortelli's scrawled hand, the cake said: 'Happy Birthday to my love, Myra'. I furrowed my brows and wondered what would possess Mama Tortelli to write such a thing. I thought back to my visit to the bakery. What had I said? I only told her to write 'Happy Birthday, Myra' on it, and she'd asked me if Myra was a little woman.

"Oh my goodness!" I said aloud, hitting my forehead with the palm of my hand. Had she asked me if Myra was '*a*' little woman or '*the*' little woman? Well, it was too late now to do anything about it. I sure hoped Myra would understand. And, more importantly, I hoped Harry would.

****

Dinner at *Woolworth* was actually quite pleasant. The three of us sat at the counter and enjoyed a surprisingly good meat loaf dinner. I went all out and ordered a root beer float with my meal…I hadn't had one in ages. It was fun watching the excitement on Myra's face, and her happiness made her look infinitely younger than her thirty-one years. She was like a kid at a carnival. As she swallowed her last bite of mashed potato, she announced that she wanted a big piece of cake. Uh oh! How was I going to get her home without blowing the surprise that I had a cake waiting for her back at the house? It was Harry who saved the day.

"Gee, Hon, I've got to make a stop by the Trib at *some* point today. We've been gone since morning. The news isn't going to write itself, you know."

Her smile disappeared.

"Now you've ruined it, Harry. I guess I don't want to keep you from your work."

She slid off the stool, stooped to pick up her packages, and started toward the front of the store. After haggling over the check, it was paid by Harry and we, too, headed the way Myra had gone. As we walked toward the exit of the store, I explained to him about the cake, faltering when I came to the greeting written atop it.

"Well, you'll see. Just remember, I didn't tell her to write that."

Harry stopped and turned to me. "Sam, don't be so worried about it. I'm not."

I followed them home in the '29 Ford. When we arrived, Harry pulled over to the curb in front of the house. I saw him lean over to kiss Myra and she got out, then he pulled away again. I parked in the drive and hurriedly exited the car to help Myra navigate the walk and steps. Under the snow were fine patches of ice in certain places making it a bit slick. It was bitter cold out and the breeze cut through like a knife. I was beginning to learn a little more about my friend, Harry. He was very short on thoughtfulness and consideration and that disappointed me. He could've made sure Myra made it inside the house before he drove away. He could've told me he wouldn't be joining us for cake. I had toyed with the idea of returning to the *Easy Street Lounge* to have another look at Eddie Killburn, but with Harry's hasty departure, I decided against that. Myra Blevins certainly didn't deserve to spend the evening all alone; especially not on her birthday.

Once inside, I helped Myra off with her coat and hung it in the closet. She was eager to show me what Harry had bought her at the store. She pulled out a navy blue dress with white polka dots and white piping around the collar. I noticed it wasn't maternity.

"Uh, I don't mean to be rude, but is that going to fit?" I gently asked.

She started to laugh. "I sure hope so. It's for after the baby is born, Sam. I want to feel pretty again after the baby is born."

I understood and nodded. Then she reached into the bag once again and pulled out a rectangle box about a half inch in height.

"And look at these, Sam. Mama and my sister, June, got these for me. I don't know how on earth they found them."

Myra took the lid off the box and gingerly lifted the contents out—a pair of real nylon stockings. She ran them through her fingers, marveling at the feel. I whistled.

"Now I want to show you something else. Close your eyes."

"Close my eyes?"

"Yep, close your eyes and here, give me your hand."

She giggled like a schoolgirl and allowed me to slowly guide her back to the kitchen.

"Alright," I said. "You can look now."

She clapped her hands together at the sight of what was on the table and said, "Oh Sam, a real rose and in the winter, no less!"

Then she read the cake. I felt uncomfortable.

"Uh, I didn't tell her to write that," I said sheepishly. "I think Mama Tortelli thought you might be my wife. Sorry about that."

"I don't care *what* it says, we've got chocolate cake! And I want two pieces!"

True to her word, Myra ate two pieces of cake and drank a large glass of milk as we sat in the living room listening to an episode of *The Lone Ranger* on the radio that was tucked in between the sofa and Harry's desk. After that came a mystery on *Suspense*.

About ten minutes into the second show, Myra was asleep. She'd had a long and exciting day and was worn out from it all. I let her sleep and continued listening to the mystery. I'd like to say I used this time to mull over the Killburn affair, but I didn't. My mind didn't leave the story that was being relayed over the wireless. Was I concerned with the fear facing Phyllis? Of course! Was I concerned that her husband might make good on his threats and attempt to kill her and possibly succeed? Most definitely, yes! But there was little I could do at the moment. I sat back in the comfortable chair and enjoyed the evening and put everything else out of my mind for the present. This was a swell birthday, even if it wasn't my own.

****

It was later on, when the house was dark and we'd all retired for the evening, that I couldn't take my mind off of the case. As I lay in bed with the quiet surrounding me, my brain raced with what I knew of these people and what I didn't know. A rush of anxiety swept the length of my body as I played Phyllis's words over and over in my head. *'I think he's going to try to kill me'. H*ow could I discover just what Eddie Killburn was up to? The only way I knew to do that was to follow him. I'd have to be up and out very early to accomplish that. Tomorrow morning, I would drive over to the Whitaker estate and perform surveillance. If I caught him driving through the gates, I'd tail him. What else was I to do? I had to know how else he spent his time, and I had to find out who he was seeing and what the relationship was. There was so much more to learn about him. My time was growing short before the dinner party, which was exactly one week from tomorrow night.

Judith White

CHAPTER ELEVEN

This was the part of the detective business that I hated the most. Not all aspects of solving crime were exciting, stimulating or a good use of time. I had to accept that.

Surveillance was a real pain in the...well, you know what. And not all surveillance brought forth the desired results. There had been many times I'd performed this sit and wait and see routine all for nothing. I truly hoped today wouldn't be one of those times.

When I woke that morning, it was still dark outside. I moved through the house quickly and quietly so as not to disturb Harry and Myra. I left them a short note explaining where I was, leaving it on the kitchen table. On my way out, I grabbed two apples from the bowl of fruit that sat on the countertop that was in between the icebox and stove. I longed for a banana, but those were almost impossible to get due to rationing. I loved bananas.

I'd eaten one of the apples more than a half hour ago and was trying to hold off on biting into the other. I'd been parked about a quarter of a mile down the road from the Whitaker drive for two hours and thirty-eight minutes now. My stomach was growling. I was hungry and I desperately wanted a cup of hot coffee. At intervals, I would start the car and allow some heat to be blown into the interior, but I had to watch that I wouldn't run myself out of gas.

It was going on 9:45 when I spotted the nose of an auto emerging from the Whitaker property. I grabbed my binoculars from the passenger seat and looked through them.

I'd never seen the man driving before. *He must be the other driver they employ*, I reasoned. He was nowhere near the size of Augie. The auto was a 1939 Rolls Royce Wraith Limousine—cream colored body with a dark green top; it was beautiful. I whistled softly. I wondered if this was one of the automobiles that Alden Whitaker had left to his daughter when he passed from this earth.

It came fully into view and turned left, away from me. I could see two people sitting in the back seat—one was Phyllis and the other was Eddie. Well, damn it all! Should I go ahead and follow, or not bother? What was going to be the sense in burning up more fuel when he obviously wasn't going to meet his girlfriend? He couldn't very well have his driver take him to his lover's residence when his wife was with him. What would he do; kiss Phyllis and tell her he would return soon, and leave her there to wait along with the driver?

I had to make up my mind quickly…give chase or abandon the tail for today? I decided not to pursue them. Instead, I had another idea.

When I'd been in the house with Phyllis yesterday, we had come up with a reason for my attending the upcoming dinner party. I would be her cousin from Detroit—a cousin she hadn't seen in a very long time. I couldn't very well walk in and introduce myself to Eddie and their friends as the detective from out of town who was hired to spy on Phyllis's husband. Yesterday, she had assured me that Augie could be trusted. He already knew she'd hired me, but he didn't know why and she knew he wouldn't ask. He was a man of few words, as I'd already found out. Brigitte would be told otherwise; that I was the cousin. All I'd have to do is stay parked here and eat my apple to use up a bit of time. Then I would make an unannounced visit to cousin Phyllis in hopes of seeing her, since I was in town. This change in course might yield nothing in the way of information pertaining to this case, but then again....

I pulled around to the rear of the house and parked. I knocked on the back door that led into the kitchen, I'd assumed. It was opened by a short, stout woman wearing a gray uniform and a white apron tied at the waist. Her hair was steel gray and short. Her face was fleshy and rather friendly looking.

"Well, hello there!" I said while smiling. "I don't believe I know your name."

Her face turned into a frown and she straightened defiantly.

"And I don't believe I know who *you* are!" she said.

Her heavy Irish brogue reminded me of my grandfather, God rest his soul.

"I'm Phyllis's cousin. Didn't she tell you I was in town?"

She didn't say a word and her eyebrows remained knit together. Obviously, her employer had neglected to mention me, and she didn't know whether to trust that I was telling the truth or not. She glanced over her right shoulder and gave someone, who was in the room along with her, a questioning look. It was Brigitte who pulled the door open wider.

"Oui. That is Madame's cousin...uh—"

"Flanagan. Sam Flanagan."

"Oui, Monsieur Flanagan."

The older woman's face softened and she broke out into a smile.

"Oh, sir, excuse me. One can't be too careful though, you know."

She moved aside and waved me in. I stepped into a kitchen that was spacious and inviting. The floor was tiled in alternate black and white squares. The appliances were white and sparkling. Something was simmering on the stove and it smelled delicious. Brigitte entered a pantry and emerged with a feather duster, and made her way out of the room.

"You just missed her, you know."

"You mean Phyllis isn't home?" I transformed my face into a look of disappointment. "Well, how about that husband of hers? I'd love to meet him. We heard she'd gotten married."

She shrugged her shoulders and lifted her hands. "I'm afraid they both went out not even an hour ago." An apology was on her face.

"Will they be back soon?"

"Afraid not. She told me not to bother with lunch because she wasn't sure they'd be here for it."

"Well, darn it all! I was so hoping to see her. Do you mind if I stay for just a bit? She might change her mind and return early."

Her face brightened and she moved nearer to help me off with my coat and hat.

"Oh, I wouldn't mind a bit of company, sir. In fact, I would love it. I don't get to see too many new faces around here. Now you just sit down at the table and I'll fix us both a cuppa."

I knew what that meant. I remembered when my grandfather was alive he'd come in from work and say, *'Ruby, girl, how 'bout fixin' your old man a nice hot cuppa?'* And my grandmother would bring him a cup of hot tea while he relaxed in his chair in the living room. The idea of steaming tea sounded wonderful. For some reason, I couldn't seem to get warm. I was chilled to the bone, probably from sitting in the Model A for hours. I watched as she took two teacups and saucers from the cupboard and set them on the table. She poured water into a kettle and turned the flame on under it. Then she removed the lid from a pot on the stove and stirred the contents.

"What are you making there?" I asked. "It smells wonderful."

Her face brightened with a wide smile.

"Good old Irish stew," she said as she tapped the ladle on the edge of the pot to loosen anything sticking to it. She replaced the lid and turned the fire under it down a notch. "What did you say your name was?" she asked as she sat across from me.

"Flanagan. Sam Flanagan," I replied.

Her face darkened. "You're not a part of the Wexford Flanagan's, are ya?"

"Not as far as I know. My grandfather was from Tralee," I answered truthfully.

She sighed and smiled. "Good thing. They're an awful bad lot."

The kettle started to boil and she rose to steep the tea. She poured the steaming water into a ceramic white teapot and brought it to the table, setting it on a hot pad. She arranged the cups in front of each of us and took her seat again.

"Your turn," I said.

She looked confused.

"You haven't told me your name," I explained.

"Oh," she laughed. "Mary. Mary Alice Mullane."

It wasn't difficult to get Mary Alice Mullane talking. She didn't receive much outside company and was thrilled to have me as her visitor. It seems she'd been employed as a cook and light housekeeper sixteen years ago. Alden Whitaker was difficult to work for. He was rude and demanding, but the pay was satisfactory and she had a son to raise. Phyllis was a bit kinder at times, although she had a lot of her father in her. After telling me this, she blushed, feeling she had been too free with information. She apologized for her indiscretion. I assured her she had said nothing wrong. I hardly knew my cousin. We'd not been in each other's lives for many years, and she had nothing to apologize for. I promised her that what was said here would not go any further. She relaxed and continued with her stories of service under this roof.

"We were all shocked when word got to us that Phyllis had married again," I said, fabricating a family bond.

"Oh, that *was* rather sudden. She hadn't known him long." She put her hand over her heart. "Oh, but Mr. Flanagan, a more decent lad you couldn't ask for. He's such a gem."

"I just want to make sure he treats her right. I guess I'm protective of family," I laughed.

Brigitte walked in at that moment, carrying the feather duster. She placed it back in the pantry. Mary rose and retrieved another cup and saucer from the cupboard.

"Come and sit a bit, girl. Have tea with us. The Killburn's won't be home for a while yet. Do ya good to have a sit down."

Brigitte accepted Mary's offer and sat at the end of the table. God, she was beautiful. If I had been Philippe, I surely wouldn't have stayed in Quebec. He was a damn fool! I couldn't help but stare at her—it was difficult to tear my eyes away. Mary lifted the lid on the teapot and decided it was time to pour. She did the honors. A bit of cream was put in each of our cups, followed by the brewed tea. She sweetened our beverages with a teaspoon of sugar, and then stirred. Brigitte stared down at her cup and placed the palms of her hands around it, as if trying to warm them. Mary sat down once again and I unwillingly tore my gaze away from the gorgeous woman sitting to my right. I took a sip of the hot liquid and savored the taste.

"It's Lyons tea," Mary proclaimed proudly.

I, once again, knew what she was talking about. My grandfather would not drink anything but this authentic Irish tea.

"Mary, if my cousin doesn't watch out, I'm going to steal you for my own."

She blushed and raised the teacup to her lips, smiling. Then she got up and went to the cupboard again and removed a bowl, and filled it with the stew. Setting it in front of me, she said, "Try that and see what ya think."

This woman was a sweetheart, and it was obvious she didn't receive what she was worth in compliments. I tasted the hot dish and told her how really delicious it was. I was being honest. It was probably the best stew I'd ever eaten. She gave me a slice of bread and set the butter in front of me before she resumed sitting across the table.

"Mary, you are too good to me. But seriously, he treats her well, doesn't he?" I said, returning to the subject of Eddie Killburn.

"Of course, he does. Oh, they've had a spat or two, just like any other couple, but nothin' to write home about," Mary answered.

Brigitte looked up and said to Mary, "Oh, Mon Dieu! Except for zat one! You remember zat?"

I was all ears.

"Ah, tis true! That was a doozy! Her screamin' at the top of her lungs and throwin' things at him. The wall got the worst of it." Mary shook her head and took another sip of her tea.

"I didn't hear it, but I had to clean up za glass and za dust za next morning." Brigitte added.

"That was just last Wednesday, right?"

I knew I'd made a mistake as soon as I'd said it. Now how would *I* know when it was? I should've kept my mouth shut and just let them tell me about Wednesday night. They both turned to me and looked at me like I was crazy.

It was Mary who spoke. "No, now why do ya say that? That was weeks ago. I could hear her screamin' upstairs. He was mainly silent, but he got in a few choice words, I suppose." She pointed to a closed door off the kitchen and said, "That's my quarters, right there. Brigitte stays in the cottage out back. She didn't hear it, but she had to clean up after it."

Brigitte nodded her head.

"Oh, I'm not sure *why* I said Wednesday."

I hung my head, shoveling stew in my mouth and hoped they wouldn't continue to wonder why I'd mentioned that particular day.

"Now that I think of it, Wednesday *was* an odd day."

I looked up at Mary.

"Really? Why is that?"

"Well, Mr. Killburn was home early. I've never known him to be feelin' ill, but that night he went to the lounge and was back by 8:15, sayin' he wasn't feelin' all that well. Do you remember, Brigitte?"

Brigitte looked at her, but just shook her head.

"Are you sure it was Wednesday?" I asked.

"Well, I was sure it was. I thought it was the day that Mrs. Killburn left early in the mornin' and didn't come home until a bit after dinnertime." She turned to the young maid again and said, "Oh, don't ya remember, girl?"

Brigitte's response was a shrug of her shoulders.

Mary continued. "But then again, you're always out of here soon after supper, back in that cottage. Anyway, maybe I'm wrong. I know one night this week he came home feelin' ill and went straight up to bed."

I finished my stew and pushed the bowl aside. I drank the last of my tea and rose from my seat.

"Well, the main thing is, he's good to her. If you say it's so, Mary, I believe you. Now I can look forward to meeting him."

She got my coat and hat and handed them to me and with a shy smile said, "I hope we can do this again, Mr. Flanagan. I've enjoyed it."

"Me, too, Mary. Me, too."

****

I drove off of the grounds and turned the way I'd come, to the right. My visit had been enjoyable. Mary Alice Mullane was a pleasant woman and an excellent cook. I was finding myself wishing Brigitte had been as talkative. Brigitte had the beauty, but Mary had the personality.

I was traveling leisurely down the road when I glanced in my rearview mirror. What I saw caused me to put on the brakes. *Was that the Rolls that just pulled into the drive at the Whitaker estate?* Well, I'll be. I didn't have a chance to see who was in the car, but I knew it was the auto that they'd left in that morning. Making a U turn, I parked along the side of the road, approximately where I'd been parked before. What were the chances that someone would leave again? What were the chances that that someone would be Eddie Killburn? I was warmer now from spending the last hour and a half indoors and sipping hot tea. My stomach was no longer growling because of eating the filling stew. What did I have to lose if I gave the surveillance another hour or so? Killing the engine, I sat back and relaxed, taking out a Lucky Strike and lighting it.

As I smoked my cigarette, I thought about the conversation that took place in the Killburn's kitchen. So they'd had a big blow out—an argument serious enough to have Phyllis throwing something at Eddie, missing him and probably taking a chunk out of the wall. An ashtray? A vase? A knick knack? Whatever it was, she was angry enough to have thrown it. Was it her suspicions of another woman? Mary and Brigitte both agreed that it had occurred some weeks ago. Mary had the idea that this past Wednesday had been the night that Mr. Killburn had returned from the lounge early, saying he didn't feel well. That was a bit unsettling to me. Mary didn't strike me as a woman who was scattered. She reminded me of a woman who remembered detail, but that was only my impression at meeting her for the first time. Brigitte couldn't confirm what day it had been because she probably was tucked away in the guesthouse at the time. Phyllis said they had a knockdown, drag out on Wednesday night: or rather very early Thursday morning. I found it funny that Mary didn't mention hearing anything, and that bothered me. I'd have to ask Phyllis if she was sure it was that night. At the time, she'd specifically mentioned it was after she'd returned from Detroit. One of them had their days mixed up.

I took another deep drag on my cigarette and then rolled the window down a crack and pitched it out into the snow. Leaning my head against the seat rest, I decided to close my eyes for a few seconds. What I wouldn't give to be able to drift off to sleep—I was getting tired. Waking so early was beginning to catch up with me now. After only a moment or two, I pried my eyes open, not trusting myself to stay awake, and saw the Super Deluxe pull out and turn left. Damn! I grabbed my binoculars and focused through the lens. Who was at the wheel? Was it this morning's driver, or was it Eddie, himself? One thing was for sure—only one person was in the car and it was a man. It wasn't Augie. Again, the man wasn't Augie's size. I started the vehicle and began to tail the sedan, keeping at a safe distance.

As I followed, the auto went through downtown Chicago and left the city, heading west. Where in the world was he going? I felt some anxiety about getting lost, but I couldn't give up now. This was another instance of a private dick wasting his time, money and energy if tailing someone didn't pan out. Finally, he pulled into a parking area in a town called Maywood. The town sat about ten miles or so outside of Chicago. I pulled up to the curb and parked across from a building that had lettering on the front stating it was the *Edward Hines, Jr. Memorial Hospital*. I had heard of this place. Back in the early '20's, Edward Hines, Sr. gave more than a million dollars to build this hospital to treat wounded war veterans. He'd lost his son in France in

WWI. He had it built in Edward, Jr.'s honor as a memorial to him.

All I could do was to wait and watch to see who would come around from the parking lot. I worried whether there was a back entrance and if the driver of the Super Deluxe would use it. There need not have been any concern though, because a few minutes later, Eddie Killburn emerged and entered the front door of the building. Now what? I couldn't very well go in there and ask what he was doing. I could always come back at a later time and do some digging then...maybe tomorrow or the day after that. Looking to my right, I noticed I was parked right in front of a diner called *The Maywood House*. Hot coffee sounded good.

I went inside and first used the facilities, then went to the cash register and asked a gentleman who was standing behind it if I could have a black coffee to go. He filled the largest container he had and I paid him. As I walked through the restaurant to take my leave, I noticed a few tables occupied by men and women dressed in medical garb.

Undoubtedly they worked across the street and were now on their lunch breaks.

As I got back into the car, I saw movement out of the corner of my left eye. I turned to look and saw Eddie Killburn exit the hospital, and he wasn't alone. He pulled the collar of his coat closer around his neck to guard against the chilly wind. His companion wore no coat. She was dressed in a nurse's uniform, and a nurse's hat was pinned to her blond hair. It was hard to tell from my perspective, but she looked young, maybe in her twenties. She wrapped her arms around herself, trying to ward off the cold. Was she crying? I couldn't tell. She had her head bent and her shoulders were shaking slightly, but that could've been in response to the frigid temperature. Eddie held out his arms and she fell into them. He held her for almost a full minute, him rubbing her back with his hands, her with her head on his shoulder. Then he kissed her on the cheek and pointed to the hospital entryway. She hesitantly reentered the building. He waved and then went around the structure and into the lot, I assumed heading toward his car.

"Well, I'll be a son of a gun," I said aloud in the car. "Gotcha Eddie Killburn!"

I started the engine and slowly pulled away from the curb. This had been a good day so far and it wasn't even half over.

CHAPTER TWELVE

Harry entered the spare bedroom and woke me to ask if I wanted to attend church with him and Myra. I declined. I'd never known him to be a churchgoer. When he and Annie were living in Detroit, she used to go every Sunday to the Bethany Presbyterian Church on West Clinton Avenue, but Harry wouldn't accompany her. Maybe Myra had been responsible for his change of heart. I would go with my grandmother occasionally, but I wasn't a regular attendee. I wouldn't have minded going with my friends, but I felt worn out for some reason. Harry didn't press me on the matter and I fell back to sleep. When I woke, I was surprised the clock on the table next to the bed said 10:20. I hadn't slept this late in months. Dragging myself out of bed, I put my pants on and headed to the bathroom to relieve myself and wash my face with cool water in an effort to wake myself further. I then headed to the kitchen to heat the coffee that had been left on the stove. There was no evidence of what Harry and Myra had eaten for breakfast, only the pot of coffee that sat on the burner. In the cupboard above the sink, I spied a box of corn flakes. I poured some into a bowl and added some raisins and milk. On the kitchen table was a copy of this morning's Chicago Tribune and I read the front page as I ate my cereal and drank the black beverage.

I read the story of British Field Marshall Viscount Gort, who was the Commander in Chief at Malta. He was seriously burned in a recent air raid while helping to salvage gasoline from a burning oil depot. He was flown back to London for treatment.

There was a short article about the Errol Flynn statutory rape trial where three women complained loudly that they hadn't been selected as jurors.

I read about a sixty two year old local Chicago man who had a row with his wife and, as a result, was locked out of his home by her at half past midnight. Out in the frigid temperature, he wore only his pajama bottoms, a robe and slippers. He woke the neighbors after forty minutes of yelling to his wife to let him in, and they called the police. The officers responding were successful in getting the woman to forgive her husband his transgression and allow him shelter within the home.

I had to laugh at that one.

The Tribune reported that today would be like yesterday as far as the weather was concerned. It was to be sunny, windy and a high of thirty-three degrees. No additional snow was in the forecast. I shivered just thinking of it. I didn't feel like going out, but I knew I had to. I wanted to return to the hospital I'd seen Eddie visit yesterday and try to find out who the woman he held outside the entryway was. A big part of this case was over, but I owed Phyllis Killburn much more than I could tell her at this point. I thought of the $1,000 and knew I would have to reimburse to her a huge chunk of it. It wouldn't hurt me to find out more than I already had and keep as much of the money as I possibly could.

I poured myself a second cup of coffee, not eager to start the day. I'd just taken my seat again when I heard the front door open. The clock just above the sink said it was only ten minutes after eleven o'clock. Did church get out this early? Usually, my grandmother didn't make it home until a bit after noon. I went to investigate and saw Myra in the process of easing down on the sofa, holding her stomach, a pained look on her face. Harry was assisting her.

"What's wrong?" I asked. "Myra, are you alright?"

Harry glanced over his right shoulder at me and said, "Sam, get one of the pillows off our bed and bring it to her."

I ran to get the pillow. We both positioned it behind her and helped her to raise her legs and recline. She turned and smiled.

"Thanks, Sam. Just a bit of crampin'."

"I don't want you on your feet today at all. You hear me, Myra?" Harry sounded frightened. "I'm calling your mother."

He left the room and headed for the phone in the kitchen.

Myra let a little laugh escape. "I felt some slight crampin' in the middle of the service and told Harry and he went all crazy. Made us leave right then and there."

"Well, I agree with him. You need to take it easy today. Stay lying down. It's better to be safe than sorry."

Harry was back within a few moments, telling us that he was going to pick up Myra's mother. Her sister, June, was at work, and would come as soon as she could.

"I'd ask you along, Sam, but I don't want Myra left alone."

I nodded.

"Oh Harry! You shouldn't have bothered June at work. I ain't crampin' now. I'm feelin' much better."

"Never mind, you heard what I said. I want you off your feet for at least today."

As soon as Harry left, I offered to fix Myra a cup of tea, and she accepted. I turned the flame on under the pot and looked through the cupboards, finally finding a few tea bags above the stove. I thought back to the tea Mary Mullane had brewed and found myself wishing she were here now. She would be a wonderful help to Myra in this situation.

I resumed sitting across from Myra in the living room. I sat in the brown print chair as she reclined on the sofa. While I had been making tea, she had snuck to her bedroom and changed from her church dress into her nightgown and robe. She was now propped against the pillow, a green afghan covering her from the waist down. She blew on her tea in an attempt to cool it a bit.

"I don't know if you can understand this, Sam. I ain't happy about this crampin' and I'm a little afraid. I don't like to see Harry scared or upset. But, in a way, I'm glad I got to see him react this way. It's nice to see he really cares, and that makes me feel good. Can you understand that?" She colored slightly with embarrassment.

"I can understand completely. Myra, Harry isn't the most considerate guy at times. I know that: I've seen it. But he's a good man. He loves you very much and he's very excited about that baby that you're carrying."

I truly believed what I had just told her.

My words made her blush and smile while she sipped at her tea. She set the cup aside on the coffee table, which I had pushed all the way up to the sofa. Gently, she slithered down further, brought the afghan up around her shoulders, and closed her eyes.

"I'm so tired, Sam," she said and yawned.

"Try to get some sleep," I urged her.

I sat and watched her sleep, and when the door opened and Harry and his mother-in-law entered, I put a forefinger up to my lips and then pointed to Myra.

"She drifted off about fifteen minutes ago," I whispered.

I rose from the chair and relieved the older woman of the bag she was carrying and took it into the kitchen. This was another example of Harry not being considerate. He could've carried the bag in from the car instead of having Myra's mother struggle with it.

"Sam Flanagan, this is Irene McKenna, Myra's mother."

I nodded. "How do you do? Very nice to meet you. Your daughter is a lovely woman."

"Well, Sam Flanagan, I think I like you already."

She smiled and started unpacking the bag that I'd set on the counter next to the sink. Irene McKenna had brought food items that, I assumed, she was going to prepare for dinner. I put half of a ham in the icebox. There was a bag of apples and some baby new potatoes. She unpacked carrots and a head of cabbage. If she were half the cook that Mary Alice Mullane was, we were in for a treat. The last thing she'd removed from the bag was a mason jar filled with a pale yellow liquid. She held it up to me.

"Chicken broth," she said. "This'll do Myra some good."

She placed it in the icebox beside the ham.

This woman had the same shade of auburn hair as Myra, only streaked with a bit of gray at her temples and by her ears. She wore it back and up in some sort of twist in the back. Mrs. McKenna was maybe two inches taller than her daughter and just as delicate looking. The one thing that marked a difference between her and her girl was the nose. Where Myra's was small and upturned, her mother's was slender, sticking out further from her face and turned downward, almost beaklike. She wore a cream-colored long sleeved housedress with muted blue flowers on it and belted at the waist. Irene McKenna was probably about ten years older than me.

After making the introductions, Harry left the room and returned to sit with Myra. I stayed and helped in any way I could. Irene found an apron hanging on a hook inside the pantry and tied it around her waist. Opening a drawer, she pulled out a paring knife and turned to me.

"How good are you at peeling apples?" she asked.

I shrugged. "I guess we'll find out."

I thought she might want to make a slaw with the apples and cabbage, but as I peeled, she began mixing flour and water. She was going to bake a pie. I didn't like the reason Mrs. Irene McKenna was here, but I was happy that she was. I loved apple pie.

****

By the time dinner was prepared, Myra had been awake for some time. She was sitting a bit more upright, listening to the radio—the music of Tommy and Jimmy Dorsey. From the kitchen, I thought I heard Edward R. Murrow interrupt the program to tell the news of the day concerning the war on the European front and in the Pacific. I'd been helping Irene where I could; peeling the apples, washing the potatoes and carrots, and setting the table. Harry had gone around the house earlier, as Myra had slept, and used the sweeper on the floors and dusted the furniture. June had arrived just about a half hour before we were to eat and had examined her sister, telling her it was probably nothing; that sometimes as a woman got closer to delivery she would occasionally experience some slight discomfort. She cautioned Myra not to do too much, though, and if the cramping returned or got severe, advised her to call her doctor. June McKenna was a few years younger than her sister, and was employed in the area as a nurse. She was still single and living with her mother. Although not a beauty, she was a pleasant looking gal. She resembled Myra, but was a taller version and not as dainty.

I set the table for three when Harry expressed his desire to eat in the living room with his wife. I didn't blame him. He wouldn't let her get up, except to use the ladie's room, and he didn't want to leave her alone. At dinner I stuffed myself and was relieved when Irene and June offered to clean the kitchen. I felt as though I couldn't move.

Shortly after eating, Myra had drifted off again and the four of us sat around the kitchen table and played Bunco, of all things, until ten o'clock that night. I'd seen my grandmother play this game dozens of times with her lady friends, but I had never learned it. Irene taught me as we went along and she wanted to play for change. She ended up walking away with forty-seven cents of my money.

****

Lying in bed that night, I thought about how I hadn't made any progress on the case. I didn't feel too bad about that though. I'd enjoyed my time with Harry's in laws. It felt like a comforting family day for me, even though this wasn't my family. And I thought about the money I was now short of. Was it possible to manipulate the game of Bunco? I wasn't sure, but somehow, and I didn't know how, I knew Irene McKenna had cheated to win.

CHAPTER THIRTEEN

I woke at 9:30 on Monday: another late morning for me. I still felt groggy. The last couple of mornings I had wanted to stay in bed all day. I felt worn out, run down. There was a dull ache sitting between my shoulders and I felt a headache crawling up from the back of my neck. I rolled out of bed, grabbing for my pants. I could hear voices coming from Harry and Myra's bedroom. I had slept in this house for five nights now and I was beginning to feel that I probably should move on—I didn't want to overstay my welcome. I got dressed and as I passed their bedroom door on the way to the bathroom, I saw Myra still in bed, propped up and leaning against two pillows. Harry was sitting on the edge of the bed next to her.

"Sam?" It was Myra's voice.

I stopped and went back to their doorway, standing just outside.

"Sam, Harry is bein' a big jerk!"

I looked at Harry with raised eyebrows, not knowing what to say.

"Sam, Myra is the most stubborn of mules!" Harry responded.

I cleared my throat. "Well, I may be a detective, but obviously I'm not that good, because I have no idea what either of you are talking about."

Myra pushed Harry out of the way and swung her feet to the floor. Sitting on the edge of the bed, she said, "He wants me to stay in bed today, and I feel just fine! He's bein' ridiculous!"

"What do you think, Sam?" Harry asked. "You think I'm being over protective? She says I am."

"I think you should trust your wife, Harry. I also think you shouldn't overdo it, Myra. And furthermore, I think I should get out of your hair. I've stayed here long enough. You two have been so generous, and I don't want to take advantage of that."

Myra's mouth dropped open and Harry just stared at me. It was Myra who spoke first.

"You ain't going anywhere."

It wasn't an invitation; it was an order.

She continued. "I mean it, Sam Flanagan. We enjoy havin' you here, and you been no trouble at all. Now don't be silly."

"She's right, Sam. You're not even done with this case. You can't leave now; in fact, you'd be doing me a favor if you stayed."

"How's that?" I asked

"Well, I can't be here all the time and neither can you. But there might be times when I'm gone and you *are* here. I'd feel more at ease just knowing that Myra wasn't alone at times. I called the office earlier and told them I'd be working from home today, but I can't do that everyday." He looked at me. "How 'bout it, Sam?"

I rubbed the back of my neck and sighed.

"As long as you feel I'm not getting under foot. Sure, I'll be happy to stay. I just didn't want to impose on you any more than I have."

Myra rose from the bed and grabbed her blue robe that was lying on a rocking chair in the corner of the room. She put it on and moved past me, shoving me and knocking me off balance.

"Aw, shut up, Sam!" she said as she continued on to the kitchen.

I turned to Harry, who was still sitting on the edge of the bed, and laughed. He put his hands in the air, palms up, and shrugged.

"Who *is* this new woman I'm married to?"

"I don't know, but I kinda like her," I said, looking in the direction Myra had gone.

****

There are times when you feel as though you are being led by divine guidance when working a case; either that, or it's just dumb luck. I'd entered the town of Maywood just before noon. I still hadn't figured out how I was going to ask about the nurse that I'd seen Eddie Killburn with. I didn't know what angle I would use. I had all the tools with me; the press pass, my binoculars and the Luger, but I had no idea what my story would be in trying to obtain information. I parked close to where I'd parked on Saturday, across from the *Edward Hines, Jr. Memorial Hospital* and in front of *The Maywood House*. I drummed my thumbs on the steering wheel while staring at the entrance of the medical facility, trying to rack my brain for an excuse to find out who this woman was. What would I say when I entered? What would I ask about her and *why*? I knew I was stalling for time, but I thought if I went into the diner, I could buy a coffee and it would help me to think. My gaze turned to the right *and there they were*! Eddie Killburn and his blond girlfriend were sitting at a table right in front of the window in *The Maywood House*. Just in case it wasn't dumb luck, I looked toward heaven and said, "Thank you!"

She wasn't in uniform today. From what I could tell, she wore some type of dark sweater and her hair was down around her shoulders in curls. She was smiling and nodding her head. Eddie reached out with his left hand and covered her right, which rested on the table. I couldn't see his face and I wanted to use my binoculars to get a better view of the situation, but I didn't dare hold them up to my eyes. Too many passersby and the couple, themselves, could look over at any second and see me. I pulled my hat down further over my eyes.

I could see her a little better than I had the other day. She wasn't bad looking; not bad looking at all. Her hair was thick and shiny and framed a lovely face. She filled the sweater out very nicely. I'd been right about her age; she appeared to be about twenty-five. I could see why he was interested. They weren't eating, as far as I could tell. She had a soda in front of her with a straw sticking out of the glass, and he didn't appear to be eating or drinking anything. She was talking now. Her hands were moving as she communicated with Eddie and then she placed them on her chest, over her heart. Whatever she was saying, it appeared to be very sincere and filled with emotion. And then she dropped her head; she appeared to be crying. Eddie rose from his chair across from her and moved to her left. He sat and put his arm around her, pulling her toward him until she laid her head on his shoulder. He was comforting her. She finally pulled away from him and took a sip of her beverage, wiping at her eyes. He said something to her which caused them both to laugh. I felt frustration at not knowing what this was all about. One thing was certain; Eddie Killburn shared a close relationship with this woman.

I started the engine, trying to warm the inside of the auto. It was bright and sunny today and the snow was starting to melt, but it was still cold outside. The driver of a car cruising at a snail's pace mistakenly thought that me starting the car was a sign that I was going to pull out, giving vacancy to a parking spot. I rolled down the window and waved him past. He stepped on the accelerator and shot past me, honking as he did so—he wasn't happy. At the sound of the horn, Eddie Killburn looked out onto the street and I hurriedly turned to my left, trying to avoid his seeing my face. I waited several moments before I turned back. When I did, he wasn't at the table; only the girl sat there now. Where had he gone? I looked both ways on the street, paranoid now that he'd seen me and exited the diner through a back way, intending to sneak up on me. I needn't have worried though, because I saw him return to the table, placing a tip on it and holding his lover's coat out for her to get into. He must've gone to the cash register to pay his bill.

I waited another ten minutes after he and the gal left the diner and crossed the street to enter the hospital. Then I got out of the car and went into *The Maywood House*. The same man as before stood behind the register. I walked up to him.

"Hi," I said. "I wonder if you can help me. I just saw a woman walk out of here with a gentleman and I'm wondering if she's who I think she is. I used to date her sister a couple years back, and doggone it, I can't remember her name now."

"*You can't remember the dame's name you used to date?*" he asked, astounded. "Brother, if you can't remember it, how am *I* supposed to help you?"

"No, no; what are you, trying to be a wise guy? I can't remember her *sister's* name." I nodded toward the door to the diner and said, "She walked out of here about ten minutes ago with a guy. She's blond, nice looking. You know who that was?"

"Only one I know of is that little gal who works across the street. She just left with some fella. I don't know her last name, but her name tag says Corinne on it when she comes in on her lunch break."

I leaned on the counter with my right elbow.

"That her boyfriend? She was seeing someone else when I was dating Pauline," I said, grabbing the name out of thin air.

He put his hands on his hips and sighed loudly.

"Now how the hell should *I* know who her boyfriend is? What are ya, *nuts*? I don't know *who* that guy is. He could be her boyfriend; he could be her brother. Hell, he could be her Dutch uncle, for all *I* know. She's been in here with him off and on for the last couple of months. And *that's* what I know! Now, you want another coffee to go or *what*?"

I straightened and looked him square in the eye.

"Are you the owner of this joint?" I asked.

"Yep."

"Then I wouldn't buy a coffee from you if this were the only diner for a hundred miles in any direction."

I turned and walked out, the owner staring after me.

****

After pulling into traffic, I headed back to Chicago. I needed to fill Harry's car with some fuel. As soon as I entered the city, I started looking for a gas station. I spotted one on the edge of town and pulled in, parking next to the pump. I told the attendant to fill it up and clean the windshield. While he did so, I went inside to use the pay phone. I dialed the Killburn residence. After two rings it was picked up by Mary.

"Hey, Mary. This is Sam. Is Phyllis there?"

"Oh, Mr. Flanagan! Might ya be comin' 'round today? I made potato soup."

"I'm not sure, Mary. If I do stop by, I might not have time for the soup. But don't you worry—I'm still working on a way of stealing you from my cousin."

She laughed and I heard her put down the phone to summon her employer. Phyllis spoke into the receiver less than a minute later.

"Mr. Flanagan? How can I help you?"

How can I help you? I held the earpiece out and looked at it, frowning. That was an odd thing to say. You would've thought she was eager for any dirt I'd discovered. I thought I was hired to help *her*!

"I have some information for you and thought I might stop by," I said.

"Information for me? What do you mean?"

I sighed heavily into the phone. *Was she kidding? Was this the same woman who dabbed her eyes with a handkerchief at my office and fretted over her husband being disloyal?*

"You *did* hire me to do a job, right? I have information about your husband."

"Oh yes, yes! I'm sorry. I'm preoccupied at the moment with trying to get to my meeting. I chair the *Greater Chicago Garden Association,* and we're meeting in less than half an hour. Could you come by, let's say, at 3:00? We can talk then, and Eddie won't be home until very late this evening."

I bet he won't, I thought. I looked at my watch. It was 12:58 right now. Sighing again, I told her I could make it. After disconnecting, I went out to the Model A. I paid the attendant with rationing stamps and then noticed what I was paying per gallon.

"Hey, when did gasoline go up to fifteen cents a gallon?" I asked him.

"It's been that price for a while now."

"Not in Detroit it hasn't," I complained.

"Yeah, well ya ain't in Detroit, buddy. You're in Chicago now."

He turned and walked into the station.

I was sick of Chicago and all the smart Alecs that lived there. And I was sick of Phyllis. There was something about that woman that got under my skin. I'd be happy when this business was finished. I'd walk into her home today and tell her about Eddie and the broad he was seeing and the job would be over. I'd refund most of her money and that would be that. There was no reason to attend that dinner party on Saturday—the investigation was complete. I'd done what I came here to do, and she could work it out from this point. She could kick him out; she could beg him to stay; I didn't care one way or the other. It was their problem, not mine. As strange as this sounded coming from a man on the precipice of becoming forty, I missed my grandmother. I'd miss Harry and Myra, and even Myra's mother when I went home, and I wished I could really take Mary back to Detroit with me. But I'd feel oh so good taking that Greyhound back to Detroit.

And then I thought about the Luger; that damned German Luger. I'd have to figure out how to get her to hand it over to me. I didn't want Phyllis Killburn dealing with all of this by putting a bullet between Eddie Killburn's eyes.

I needed a couple of stiff drinks and I knew where to get them. I headed toward Michigan Avenue and the *Easy Street Lounge*.

Chapter Fourteen

The place was virtually empty; only one other drinker sat at the bar. The woman had a mug of beer in front of her and she was smoking a small cigar. She was short and wrinkled, and looked about sixty-five, but I had a funny feeling she was only about forty-five but wearing all the years of bad habits. She still had her heavy coat on and wore a stocking cap, covering her hair. Every time I looked in her direction, I caught her staring at me, and she'd smile and wink. Her two front bottom teeth were missing—I tried to avoid looking at her.

"Come on, Vi. Be a good girl and finish your beer and mosey on home to your old man," Turk said. "You've been in here long enough, and he must be missing you by now."

The bartender was washing glasses, dipping them in one sink filled with suds and then immersing them in the adjacent sink that held clear, hot water. He was dressed in a short-sleeved white shirt with black pants and an olive green bow tie. A long green apron was tied at his waist. Turk was about my age. He was slender and of average height. His hair was thinning on top and he wore a mustache. The one outstanding characteristic about him was that he had a scar running from his left cheekbone to just short of the corner of his mouth, like someone had cut him. It must have been one hell of a fight.

Surprisingly, Vi did as she was told and guzzled the last of her drink and slid off the stool, taking her purse and cigar with her. Her departure from the lounge was unsteady.

I looked at Turk and said, "She gonna be alright?"

"Oh yeah," he replied. "She just lives around the block. She's in here everyday like clockwork."

"Give me another, Turk," I said, sliding my empty glass over to him.

"Hey, you know my name?" He looked surprised.

"I heard it the other night. I was in here for dinner on Thursday," I said.

He broke out into a smile and waved his forefinger in my direction.

"Right, right! Sat in the booth over there."

He pointed toward where I had sat. I nodded. He handed me another scotch on the rocks and I took a sip. He went back to washing glasses. What he said next startled me.

"You guys can't fool me. I know what you were doing here; checking out Eddie. I can spot you guys a mile away."

"How's that?" I asked.

"That was probably your partner who was here right before Christmas. You know, the record deal. Eddie is good, huh?"

"Record deal?" I asked.

He stopped washing the beer mug and dried his hands on a towel. He leaned his elbows on the bar in front of me.

"Don't tell me you guys don't want him now?"

I started to relax. I'd been checking Eddie out on Thursday night, but not for the reason he thought. I pulled out a cigarette and Turk tossed me a pack of matches from behind the bar. I lit it and inhaled deeply.

"You're losing me, Turk. I have no idea what you're talking about," I said, truthfully.

Turk went on to tell me that a talent agent had spotted Eddie and talked to him about auditioning out in L.A.; a record deal might possibly be in the works for him. I had to admit that Eddie was good enough—at least, *I* thought he was. What an opportunity for the young man! With his talent and his good looks, he would go far.

"Well, now that I know you aren't from L.A., I can tell you that I doubt that will ever be in his future," Turk said, and he shook his head. "With everything that kid does for others, he could've used some good fortune himself. Now he can't even grab on to this deal."

"Why not?"

"Eh, Eddie comes in the night after the guy was here and he was very upset. Seems he told his wife about the offer and she threw a holy tantrum. She wanted no part of the possibility of them moving out to L.A. So, case closed. But that isn't what upset him so much. It's that she busted some type of urn during the big blow out that belonged to him. It was handed down to him by his mother, who got it from *her* mother. Seems when his grandmother came here from the old country, she brought *her* mother with her. *In the urn*! Eddie's great grandmother was *in that urn*!"

I stared at him blankly. I didn't get it and I told him so.

"*Cremation*," he said. "And if you ask me, that's kind of creepy. It just isn't natural."

****

During the drive to the Whitaker estate, I still couldn't get the thought of that argument that took place some weeks ago out of my mind. I wondered if Brigitte knew that she not only cleaned up glass shards, but Eddie Killburn's great grandmother as well. An involuntary shudder ran through me. I pulled into the drive and parked in front. Mary answered my knock. She had a broad smile on her face and she waved me in.

"You've got the worst timin'," she said, as she took my coat and hat.

"You mean she isn't here?"

I looked at my watch. She had told me to be here at 3:00 and it was now ten minutes after the hour; my lame attempt to get back at her for making me wait when Augie had picked me up from Harry's.

She shook her head and told me the lady of the house neglected to say what time she would return.

"Can I just wait in there?" I nodded toward the huge living room where I'd waited for Phyllis before.

Mary lost her smile. I'd hurt her feelings with not wanting to join her in the kitchen.

"I don't want to bother you, but I'd rather have your company, if you aren't too busy," I said, trying to make amends.

That did it. The smile returned and she told me she'd love it if I joined her.

When we entered the kitchen, there was old newspaper spread across the table. On it sat a half dozen silver candlesticks and a few ornate silver bowls. Silver polish and a rag sat nearby. Mary had been restoring their shine. I took a seat at the table.

"Phyllis told me she would be home by 3:00," I said. "Her gardening meetings usually last this long?"

"Gardenin' meetin'? No, those don't start until late March. She got a call from a gentleman and high tailed it outta here. Somethin' put her in a good mood. Got the call right before yours, Mr. Flanagan."

"Ah, I might've misunderstood her," I lied.

What was this dame pulling? No matter *where* she went, why make up some story? I didn't care where she went. It was odd, and I was irritated by it.

I sat and watched Mary polish. I thought I would give Phyllis ten minutes and then I would leave and give her a call later on to tell her the news about her adoring husband. And then, I would make plans to leave and go back to Detroit. I'd mail her a check for the refund of most of her retainer. Five of the ten minutes went by and the phone rang. Mary excused herself and went out of the kitchen to wherever the phone was located. She returned a moment later.

"Mrs. Killburn is on the phone and wants to talk to ya."

She led me into another large living area and left me alone to talk to Phyllis.

"Mr. Flanagan, I am so sorry I didn't make it home in time. The meeting ran longer than I thought. I'll still be here for about another hour. Maybe you can tell me on Saturday at the dinner party."

So she was still clinging to the lie she'd told me. What did I care? I didn't let on that I knew differently.

"I found out what you wanted to know," I said. "He's involved with some woman named Corinne and she's a nurse. I don't know her last name but they seem to be pretty close. There's really no need for me to see you on Saturday. I can always send you the portion of the money I didn't earn."

There was dead silence on the other end.

"Phyllis?"

Nothing. I thought she'd hung up or we'd been disconnected. And then I heard the faintest of whispers.

"Are you sure? I don't believe you."

"Look, Phyllis, I know this isn't easy. But you suspected it, otherwise why come to me? I am so sorry. I know you were hoping to hear something different."

"There must be some mistake. *There must be*!" She'd found her voice. "Look, we can discuss this further on Saturday."

"Didn't you hear me? I've done the job you hired me to do. Why should I attend your party? There's really no need."

"You have to be there! You *have* to! I don't care about the money. We have to talk further about this."

****

This had been an unsettling day. I woke tired and I felt as though I was dragging now. I was glad to be back at Harry's and relaxing in the chair, listening to him peck away on his typewriter and watching Myra knit something for the baby as she sat on the couch. Harry pulled the paper from the machine and went to the kitchen. When he returned, he handed me a glass of scotch while holding one for himself. I told them about my odd day, starting with spotting Eddie with the nurse from the *Edward Hines, Jr. Memorial Hospital. I* told them all of it—from the diner owner to the odd behavior that Phyllis had displayed, and how she'd gotten me to stick to my promise of attending her dinner party.

"Well, gee, Sam. All you have to do to find out about this woman is ask June," Myra said.

I cocked my head to one side and said, "Ask June?"

"That's right," Harry added. "She works at that hospital. I thought she might have mentioned that to you last night."

Judith White

CHAPTER FIFTEEN

By the time I'd opened my eyes on Tuesday, Harry had been long gone to the Trib. When I made my way to the kitchen, there was a note on the table telling me that Myra had gone to her mother's and wouldn't be home until just before dinnertime. I picked up the morning edition of the Chicago Tribune that was next to Myra's note and took it back to the bedroom with me. I got back in bed and started to read an article about the enemy bombing of U.S. positions on Guadalcanal Island, but I never finished it. I had fallen back to sleep. It wasn't a peaceful sleep. I had a dream in which I was being chased by someone holding a German Luger. I kept telling the woman next to me to run faster. It was Phyllis, but she kept resisting me, telling me she loved this man and wanted to be with him. When I turned to see who was shooting at us, I saw Augie holding the gun. I woke drenched in sweat. Not only was I perspiring, but I felt weak and achy. When I swallowed, my throat felt like it was closing up. It was 1:20 in the afternoon, but I just rolled over and closed my eyes again.

****

"Hey, buddy. Wake up."

I forced my eyes to open and saw Harry in the dimness. The sun was going down and it provided just enough light in the room to make him out. My God, how long had I slept?

"Can you get up for a bit? Myra wants to change the sheets. They're all damp. I've got some clean pajamas of mine for you to wear."

I grunted and tried rolling out of bed. Taking the clothing that he was holding out to me, I headed for the bathroom. I was sweating, but I shivered with chills. Once in the room, I turned on the faucet, running myself a tub of hot water, desperate to get warm. The heat seemed to soothe some of my achiness. I lay back in the water and only my face was above the surface. It felt wonderful, but I still couldn't stop shaking. I must've lain there about twenty minutes before I washed my hair and scrubbed my body. I wanted to add more hot water and just ease back again, but I was afraid I would fall asleep in the tub.

Harry's pajama bottoms were a bit too long on me, even though around the waist they were fine. The top fit me well. I emerged from the bathroom feeling a tad better and asked him if I could use the phone to check on my grandmother. The clock above the sink told me it was 5:45. It would be 6:45 back home. She picked up on the second ring.

"Gran, this is Sam," I said a bit louder than usual into the phone.

"Oh, hi, Sam. How's your case coming along? And why are you speaking so loud?"

I was amazed. Was this my grandmother? She sounded coherent and *normal*.

"It's going fine. I just thought I would call to see how you are doing. Is everything alright at home?"

"Everything is good. The boys from next door are over and I had a bit of sugar so we are baking peanut butter cookies," she told me. "You don't sound too well, though. Is something the matter, dear?"

How I wished I were home to have some of those cookies. It just didn't seem fair that she was actually baking; something she didn't do quite as often as she used to, and I wasn't there. I found myself resenting Albie and Bobby. For a man who was more than triple their age, I was feeling pretty juvenile. But I had to push my infantile jealousy aside and recognize that having those boys around was good for my grandmother.

I told her I was coming down with a cold or something and asked her to put Albie on the phone.

"Hey, Mr. Flanagan," he greeted me. "We're makin' cookies!"

"Have you been doing what I paid you to do?"

"Yep!"

"Good. There's another quarter in it for you when I get home if you can not only read the mail to her, but go over and visit her every so often, too. What do you think? Can you do that?"

"Sure! She already invited us over for supper tomorrow and Ma said we could. But Mr. Flanagan?"

"What?"

"What about Bobby? He'll need another quarter, too."

****

I returned to the bedroom, shutting the door. I sure didn't want to have Myra coming down with whatever I was getting. An extra blanket had been laid across the bed. Crawling under the covers, I thought about how Albie was becoming quite the little negotiator and con man. I closed my eyes and fell into a fitful sleep.

Wednesday was a repeat of Tuesday. Waves of fever and chills alternately washed over my body. Myra had made homemade chicken soup, but there was little chicken in it. She served me some for lunch and then brought in some more at supper time. The broth felt good on my throat. She'd been without coffee for the past two days, so she served me cups of weak tea because she was running low on that, too. The whole country was suffering the effects of rationing. Everyday items we all used to enjoy were sparse or even impossible to get. I was feeling very guilty for helping to deplete Harry and Myra's supply of goods. The only rationing stamps I'd brought with me were the ones I had for gasoline. My grandmother didn't need them because she didn't drive, but I'd left all others for food goods with her. I was now wishing I could contribute. The only thing I could think of to do was to leave a little money behind when I boarded that bus back to Detroit.

On Wednesday night, just before going to bed herself, Myra came in holding a teaspoon with some kind of tonic in it and a glass of water.

"I talked to June and she told me to give you this."

"What is it?" I asked.

"Just never mind. You don't wanna know."

I didn't ask again. I opened my mouth and she inserted the spoon. I licked it clean and then, holding the substance in my mouth, I looked around for a place to spit it. My face curled up with the awful taste of it.

"Don't you dare!" she said to me. "Swallow it!"

I did and reached desperately for the glass of water. I guzzled it until it was gone.

"My God!" I exclaimed, wiping my mouth with the sleeve of Harry's pajama top.

Myra was laughing as she turned and left the room, closing the door after her.

****

Whatever was in that tonic Myra had given me, it had helped tremendously. I woke on Thursday without a fever. The chills were gone. The pajamas I wore, and the sheets, were dry. I looked heavenward and silently mouthed my gratitude. When I moved to leave the bed, I noticed my body still ached slightly, and I still felt a little weak. But I was so much better than I had been for the last two days.

I found Myra sitting on the sofa, knitting. Whatever she was making, it contained yellows and greens. She held it up for me to see.

"It's a sweater. I knitted a matching bonnet."

I nodded.

"That stuff you gave me last night; it sure did the trick. Although I'm not 100%, I feel so much better," I told her.

She smiled and rose and headed for the kitchen.

"You should still take it easy today. I'm gonna make you some tea."

While she put the kettle on, I went back into the bedroom and took the extra blanket off the bed. I returned to the living room and sat in the chair, covering my legs with it. Staring out the front window, I watched as a train slowly made its way along the tracks. Drips of water fell to the ground from the eaves lining the front of the house. The sun was bright, and the snow was melting. As I continued to watch the train, Myra brought me the cup of tea and two slices of buttered toast, and I thanked her. As I ate the toast and sipped at the hot beverage, I noticed a magazine sitting on the end table next to the chair. I browsed through the pages and came across an advertisement for men's hair tonic. In the ad the gentleman wore an expensive looking tuxedo, and I groaned inwardly. Why had I agreed to attend that party on Saturday? Phyllis told me it was very formal, and I didn't have the clothing that I knew I should wear. I leaned my head on the back of the chair, closed my eyes and sighed. Oh well, what could I do? I didn't feel well enough to shop for something suitable, and besides, I doubted there was time for that. With alterations, I doubted a new suit or tuxedo would be ready by Saturday evening. And another road block was that not only food, but clothing, too, was in short supply.

"What's the matter, Sam?" Myra asked, as she pulled more green thread from her ball of yarn.

I voiced my predicament and added how angry I was at myself for allowing Phyllis Killburn to manipulate me. Myra didn't say a word. She set her knitting aside, got up from the sofa, and left the room. When she came back, she was holding up a black tuxedo on a wooden hanger, a black bow tie dangling from its wire hook. I just stared at it.

"It's Harry's," she said. "Last September he had an awards dinner and got it then. He got some award for journalism."

She smiled, proudly.

"I can't wear that, Myra. You two have done enough for me already."

She brushed my objections aside and told me all she would have to do is hem the pants. She could always let the hem out later, after I'd worn it. She told me I didn't even have to try them on because she would measure them according to the length of my own suit pants. I didn't fight her further on it because, to tell the truth, I wasn't feeling up to the arguing.

Myra went to the hall closet and got her coat. Putting it on, she told me she was going next door to see if her neighbor had black thread she could borrow, and she told me not to worry if she didn't return right away—she just might decide to stay for a while and visit.

I stayed in the chair and snoozed as the sun entered the living room, providing comforting warmth. I was relaxed and feeling at ease. A half hour went by and I heard the phone ring. I went to the kitchen and answered it.

"Hello? Blevins residence," I said.

"Well, hello, Mr. Flanagan. And how are you feeling this afternoon? We heard you were ill."

I recognized the voice. It was Myra's mother, Irene McKenna. I told her I was feeling better and she asked to speak to Myra. I explained where Myra was.

"Mrs. McKenna, I'm very glad you called. I've wanted to get hold of June to ask her something. She wouldn't happen to be home, would she?"

"Yes, she's here. I'll put her on, but just tell Myra I called when she comes in."

I agreed to do that and waited while she summoned the daughter who lived with her. June spoke breathlessly into the mouthpiece.

"Hello?"

"June, I hope I'm not disturbing you. This is Sam Flanagan. I wanted to ask you something."

"Yes, mother told me you were on the phone. I'm just rushing to get ready for work. What can I help you with?"

I then told her that I'd learned she worked with a woman named Corinne, but I didn't know her last name.

"That would be Corinne Schneider. Nothing is wrong, is it?"

"No, no," I assured her. "It's just that I saw her with Eddie Killburn the other day—"

She cut me off by saying, "Oh yes! He's been so wonderful to her. I don't know what she would do without him. She just loves him to pieces!"

"Well, just between the two of us, June, you know he's married and—"

She cut me off again.

"Yes, I know that. She does, too. She's grateful for any time he can give her. They've really hit it off. She'd do anything for that man and...." She stopped for a moment and then continued, "Oh, Mr. Flanagan, I've really got to be going. I just noticed the time. I hope you don't think I'm rude."

"No, not at all," I said.

"Thank you so much. Have a great day now," she said.

I heard a click in my ear. She'd hung up.

I replaced the receiver and went back to the chair in the living room, pulling the blanket up around me. That was strange. June knew he was married and so did Corinne, yet June didn't seem to think that was a problem. What was this world coming to? I wondered if Corinne was not only Eddie Killburn's lover, but his partner in crime as well. It hadn't been lost on me that her last name was Schneider: a very German last name.

Judith White

CHAPTER SIXTEEN

"You look absolutely killer-diller!" Myra exclaimed.

"Hmm, that good, huh?" I laughed.

It was Saturday evening and I was dressed in Harry's tuxedo. Myra had hemmed the pants to the perfect length. I was ready to make my appearance at the Whitaker estate, tonight's location for the dinner party which Phyllis and Eddie Killburn were hosting. I didn't even really know why I was going. What was I going to learn that I hadn't already? What could I tell Phyllis that I hadn't already told her? Except for Corinne's last name, there was nothing else to reveal. The case, as far as I was concerned, was over. Yet, I had promised Phyllis that I would put in an appearance and that's what I would do. We never agreed I had to stay the duration of the event.

I grabbed my overcoat and picked up the keys that were sitting on the coffee table.

"I guess we won't wait up for you," Harry joked.

I smiled.

****

When I pulled into the drive at the estate, two men were standing near the entrance waiting to accept the keys to the vehicles and park them. One was Augie and one was their other driver. I got out, leaving the car running, and the man I'd never met entered and pulled the Model A around back. In passing Augie, I uttered a greeting and he said nothing. I knocked on the front door and it was immediately opened by Mary. She gave me one of her warm smiles.

"Oh, Mr. Flanagan, aren't we lookin' dapper this evenin'?"

I smiled and bent down to kiss her on the cheek. She blushed and took my coat and hat. I spied Phyllis coming toward me. The woman looked really beautiful tonight, wearing a floor length red gown that highlighted her skin tone and curves. When she walked, the dress flowed behind her. She put her arm through mine and kissed me lightly on the cheek, which startled me a bit. I had to remind myself that this would be completely natural behavior for cousins.

"Sam!" she greeted me. "I am so glad you could make it!"

"Phyllis, you look lovely," I responded.

I didn't think using the term 'killer-diller' would be appropriate for this group of people.

We entered the living area that I'd been guided to when I'd first come to the estate. People had already arrived and were standing and talking with drinks in hand. Phyllis made the rounds with me, introducing me to her other guests. I met Captain and Mrs. Ross; he was in his Army dress uniform. I was introduced to a Major and Mrs. Brock. He, too, was wearing his finest military attire. First Lieutenant Ronald Fitzroy greeted me and told me his wife was feeling ill and had decided to stay home at the last minute. Phyllis introduced me to Dr. Dabney Harrell and his wife, Enid. The one remaining couple was the longtime friends of Phyllis, Wilmer and Iona Cosgrove, the couple who had hosted the Killburn's wedding reception almost a year and a half ago. To all of them, she presented me as her cousin on her mother's side that was now living in Detroit. Eddie was over in the corner at the piano, playing a soft tune I didn't recognize. Phyllis led me to him and he stood, reaching for his martini that had been sitting on top of the instrument. He took a sip and then extended his right hand.

"Well, you *have* to be Sam. I've been eager to meet you."

He had a firm grip and he flashed his smile, exposing his one dimple. Everything about this guy radiated charisma. I found myself drawn to him from the get go. Who could meet Eddie Killburn and *not* immediately like him? I could see why Phyllis would feel the attraction, even though the age difference stood between them. He stepped out from behind the piano and put his arm around me, leading me a few steps away, dragging his left leg as he went along. He signaled to Brigitte to bring me a drink. He asked me all the normal questions; how were things in Detroit, what was Phyllis like as a child, what did I do for a living. I told him lies upon lies and didn't feel good about doing it. There was something about this young man that was very warm and genuine. We stood and talked a few more moments, and then we all moved into the other living area of the house and found several trays of hors d'oeuvres set out on a buffet. This was the room that I'd entered earlier in the week to speak to Phyllis on the phone. I looked around, taking in more of the décor. It contained two green and gold print sofas and a half dozen solid green chairs. Various decorative tables were placed around the room and a beautiful bar with ornate carvings stood at the far end. Paintings lined one wall and directly opposite was the massive front window looking out onto a yard filled with tall pine trees. The drapes were wide open and I noticed it had begun to snow. This was a spectacular house!

I was standing alone, off to the side, when the First Lieutenant came up to me asking if I'd ever served in the military. I answered him honestly, telling him no. I'd been too young when the United States had gotten involved in the Great War back in 1917. I was only fourteen at the time. We exchanged a few pleasantries before being joined by Major Brock.

"Ron, Adelaide isn't feeling well? Am I correct in hearing you say that?" Brock asked.

"One of her migraines. I'm sure she's trying to sleep it off. Ted, you've been introduced to Phyllis's cousin, haven't you?" he gestured to me.

"Yes," Ted Brock nodded in my direction, then turned and resumed his conversation with Ronald Fitzroy.

A snub? I thought

"You heard the comment made this week by Obersturmbannfuhrer Reinhardt, didn't you? That damn Nazi is an absolute lunatic!"

"As they all are, Ted. There's no doubt about that."

"Patton's complaining loudly again," Ted Brock said and then sipped his drink.

"You'll never shut George Patton up! But he's one hell of a general, Ted. No one can fault him for his strategy and tactical planning, that's for sure. What is it this time?"

I quietly eased away from the two men; I doubted they noticed. My gaze swept the room. Eddie was over by the bar speaking to Wilmer Cosgrove and Mrs. Brock. Captain Ross and his wife were by the window looking outside. The captain was pointing at something in the yard. His wife was looking up at him as he spoke and her face was filled with love and admiration. Dr. Dabney Harrell didn't appear to be in the room. Phyllis stood with Enid Harrell, the doctors' wife, and her friend, Iona Cosgrove. She was speaking animatedly with her hands moving through the air and the other two women were laughing. I headed in their direction. It was nice to see Phyllis enjoying herself. She appeared to be very happy tonight. As I approached, she sipped her red wine and waved me over. When I arrived, she slipped her arm through mine again.

"Don't I have the most handsome cousin, ladies?"

They both smiled and I felt that Enid Harrell held her gaze on me a little too long. She was a short woman in her forties, who carried an extra twenty or thirty pounds she didn't need. Her black hair was swept up on top of her head and blossomed into a crown of curls. The beige gown that she wore seemed to blend in with her skin tone, and it wasn't flattering. Her large brown eyes bore right through me, and I could've sworn she winked. I turned my gaze away. I leaned over toward Phyllis, pretending to kiss her on her cheek, but whispered in her ear instead. I asked her when we could talk. She didn't respond directly to my question, but instead announced to me and the two ladies that we could go to the dining room, it was time for dinner.

It was 8:00 and we took our places around the table. Phyllis directed me to sit between Enid Harrell, who was to my left, and Wilmer Cosgrove, who was to my right. The table was set with beautiful crystal, polished silver and fancy napkins. A few days ago, I would've been impressed with all of it, but I found myself getting bored with such things now. This lifestyle didn't hold the same appeal that it first did. I no more fit into Phyllis Killburn's world than she did mine.

The first course was a French onion soup, followed by Cornish hens with carrots and asparagus and some sort of potato cake that contained heavy cream and cheese. A carefully selected white wine was served with the meal. Throughout dinner, Enid Harrell tried several times to strike up a conversation with me, but it didn't work. I wasn't trying to be rude, but I had nothing in common with her; I didn't know what to say to her. At one point she laid her hand on my left thigh and began to rub.

"Have you ever been to Sao Luis, Sam?"

She was deliberately trying to make her voice sound sensuous. She couldn't pull it off.

I replied, "Where?"

"Sao Luis. It's in Brazil, silly."

Her husband, sitting to her left, cleared his throat loudly and she pulled her hand away and resumed eating.

Dessert was a light chocolate mousse with raspberries on top. There were no signs of rationing displayed in this household.

****

We returned to the large room containing the bar where coffee and additional cocktails were being served. I opted for the coffee; I hadn't had a cup for days. The paintings along the wall drew my attention and I stepped up to them, wanting to get a closer look. The first was of a little blond girl swinging on a swing that was hanging from the branch of a huge oak tree. A barn was in the far distance and grass and wildflowers covered the ground. The next was a painting of the English countryside. Three cottages looked out onto a canal. Families of ducks were gliding across the water. As I studied it, I didn't hear Eddie Killburn come up behind me.

"It was a wedding gift from Phyllis. Your cousin knows me through and through. She always seems to know what's important to me," he said. "It reminds me of my days in England. I love it. It's an original, you know. It's beautiful, isn't it?"

I nodded in agreement and then bent to see the artists' signature more clearly. It was a name I didn't recognize.

"Oh, I doubt you'll know of the painter. He lives in Liverpool," he added.

As I was still stooped, Dr. Harrell put his hand on Eddie's arm and asked him if they could talk. Eddie excused himself, but they only moved a couple feet away. I paid no attention to their conversation until I heard the name Corinne mentioned. I pretended to still study the artwork but, in reality, strained to hear what was being said.

"Oh, she's great, Dab. And she's actually the stronger of the two. She's going to be of so much support. There's something about Corinne, and I just can't put my finger on it."

"Mark my words, Eddie; it's a time bomb waiting to happen."

For God's sake, how many people knew about this love affair? At least the doctor had the common sense to oppose it in his own way. What support would Corinne offer Eddie that Phyllis hadn't supplied? And then I thought back to Turk and his mentioning the record deal that was going to possibly be offered to Eddie. Is that what he was talking about? Would he leave Phyllis and move out to L.A. with Corinne? Take his current love with him in pursuit of a whole new life and career?

I looked around the room and saw Phyllis standing by herself behind the bar. She appeared to be mixing a drink. I walked over to her and stood in between two stools.

"We need to talk. I won't be here that much longer," I said.

Phyllis looked up, a bit startled—she hadn't seen me approach. Putting down the shaker she'd been holding, she didn't say a word.

"Look, Phyllis, I know this is very difficult for you. It's not the end of the world, though. You two can work it out," I lied. "The gal's name is Corinne Schneider."

I didn't want to go into detail and tell her everything I'd seen and heard. Why twist the knife when you've already got it buried up to the hilt?

It was at that point that Brigitte walked up to us.

"Excuse me Madam, but zere was a call from New York. He said he would call back because he didn't want to interrupt your gazzering."

She walked away, Phyllis staring after her. She turned to me and it was as if all the blood had drained from her face.

She whispered, "How can he do this? How can he do this to me? I *trusted him, Sam*!"

Her eyes started to water and she hung her head. I didn't know what to say. Whenever I had to deliver bad news and witness its effect, that was when I'd thought I'd made a wrong choice in careers.

"I'm sorry, Sam. I need a few moments to compose myself."

"I understand," I said and I backed away.

I took my almost empty coffee cup and headed for the kitchen. I found Mary at the sink, washing dishes. She looked over at me as I entered.

"Now what are ya doin' in here, Mr. Flanagan? You should be out with the others havin' a high time of it."

"I came to tell you that you hit another home run, Mary. That dinner was the best!" I held up my coffee cup. "I also came for a refill. Where I'm staying; well, we've been out for a few days. I thought I'd take advantage of the situation." I winked at her.

She dried her hands on a towel and opened a cupboard to her right. She pulled down a glass canister filled with coffee grounds. She then filled a small brown paper bag with the commodity.

"I'll just put this in your coat pocket; and remember, mum is the word."

"You're a doll, Mary. If I were an older man, would you consider marrying me?"

She laughed and put her hand over her heart. Then she straightened in mock defiance.

"And just what makes ya think I'm so much older than you are, Mr. Flanagan? No, no; the next man I marry has to have lots and lots o' money; and you ain't him!" She laughed again.

I gave an exaggerated look of sadness and told her she'd broken my heart.

She waved the towel at me and said, "Oh, now get goin' ya fool!"

I heard her begin to laugh again as I left the kitchen with a full cup of steaming coffee.

Looking around the room, I didn't see Phyllis. No doubt she was up in her room pulling herself together, trying to recuperate from the bad news she was now starting to believe. What was it Charlie Kuntz had said about Jack Calvert marrying her for her money? Something about how she would've never believed it. I felt sorry for her.

People were still mingling, still drinking. I moved over to the sofa, setting my cup and saucer on the table in front of me. Lighting a cigarette, I gazed out the window and watched the flakes fall from heaven. Beautiful piano music floated in from the next room. Eddie was playing *Somewhere Over the Rainbow,* and he was singing to it.

Gran would've enjoyed being here to hear it; she loved the song. It was during the next number, *Puttin' On The Ritz* made famous by Fred Astaire, that Captain Ross and his wife came and sat next to me on the sofa.

"So how are things in Detroit, Sam?" the Captain asked. "We used to live there."

"Is that right? Well, probably about the same as everywhere else. Jobs are still tough to come by in some ways. People just trying to make it despite the war and rationing."

He nodded in his wife's direction.

"Lillian has a brother just north of the city. A place called Flint. You know it?"

"Oh yeah, I've been there," I answered.

"We both liked it there, didn't we, Charles?" Lillian said.

"Oh yeah, sure did. We were there back in '22 and '23; a couple of pretty good years for the Tigers."

"Yep, yep. Ty Cobb was playing then. Not much of a personality, but he could sure play ball. I miss him," I added. "I wonder what he's doing now."

"Probably went back to Georgia," Charles Ross said.

He went on reminiscing about their time in Detroit. As he talked, I looked past him and saw Dr. Harrell enter the room where Eddie was playing. The music stopped for a few moments and when the doctor returned, the songs started up again. About ten minutes later, Major Brock went to talk to Eddie. I saw Phyllis come down the stairway and head toward the bar. She had pulled herself together—there was no evidence of her crying. I hadn't seen Major Brock reenter the room, but when I turned to look at Phyllis again, he was there talking to her. It was time for me to make an exit. I sipped at my now lukewarm coffee and decided I would definitely leave when the cup was empty.

Suddenly, Brigitte let out a high-pitched scream, causing me to jump, spilling my coffee all over Harry's tuxedo and splashing some on the captain's uniform. I couldn't tell where the scream had come from, but Dr. Harrell was on his feet in seconds and was running toward the piano room. The rest of us just sat there looking at each other for a moment. Then I was on the move. The others followed me. What I saw shocked me. It was a sight I will never forget.

Eddie Killburn sat on the couch nearest the fireplace, his head resting against the back cushion. His left arm was dangling over the side and his hand hung just above the martini glass that he'd let fall to the carpet. As if he'd tugged at it, trying desperately to remove it, his bow tie was all askew. The young man's face was twisted into an agonizing grimace, and his eyes were staring blankly toward the ceiling, seeing nothing. The future for the husband of Phyllis Killburn didn't exist anymore. His talent and charisma were things of the past. Eddie Killburn was dead.

CHAPTER SEVENTEEN

No one moved for some seconds. No one, except the doctor, realized what they were looking at. Dr. Dabney Harrell was hunched over the body with the tips of his fingers resting against Eddie Killburn's throat. He straightened and looked back at the rest of us. He removed his round black framed glasses from his face and began cleaning them with a handkerchief he'd retrieved from his pocket. His head was bent and he shook it slightly. One of the women behind me gasped.

"What happened? Was it a heart attack?" she asked.

Phyllis pushed her way through those in front of her and stopped when she saw Eddie's lifeless body. She looked at the doctor with a questioning look and then she bolted forward, falling to her knees in front of her husband.

"Eddie? Eddie, dear, what is it?"

She began roughly shaking his leg. I moved forward and helped her to stand. She faced me and cocked her head to the side.

"I don't understand, Sam! What's wrong with him? *What's wrong with him?*"

She began crying and beating her fists against my chest. I brought her in closer, holding her tight. I turned to the crowd.

"For God's sake! Someone call the police and an ambulance!" I yelled with anger.

It was Captain Charles Ross who bolted from the room, heading for the telephone. His wife had her arm around a sobbing Brigitte. She led the maid into the next room.

"Everyone out," I said. "Touch nothing."

The crowd was retreating into the other room and I heard one of the men say they needed another drink. I called to Iona Cosgrove to stay behind. She walked up to Phyllis and me. Phyllis was crying uncontrollably.

"Take her into the other room. Get her a drink if you have to," I ordered.

She nodded and put her arm around her friend and led her away. I turned to the doctor. I asked him if he had any idea what had happened. He shook his head.

"No idea at all. Too early to tell," he answered.

I looked beyond the doctor to Eddie Killburn's body. His face was contorted with his last moments of agony and it pained me to see him this way. The right corner of his mouth was tinged blue, and so were some of his fingernails near the cuticle. I turned to Dr. Harrell again.

"What would cause that?" I asked.

"Lack of oxygen. There might be other causes, but it's too soon to say." He nodded toward the doorway.

"We should wait out there until help arrives," he said somberly.

As we were exiting, Mary was heading toward us.

"Is it true, Mr. Flanagan?" she asked, her eyes beginning to water.

I nodded my head and put my arm around her, guiding her away from the scene of the body.

"I'm afraid so, Mary. You might want to put on another pot of coffee," I suggested.

She stopped in her tracks and made a sign of the cross. She bent her head and started to weep quietly, and made her way to the kitchen without another word. In the room where the others were located, I looked for Phyllis. She was sitting on the sofa next to Iona Cosgrove, still crying.

"I don't understand it," she cried. "Why would he leave me? What made him go? I trusted him! Why would he leave me? *Not again*!"

Iona pulled Phyllis closer to her and rocked back and forth, trying to soothe her friend. Lillian Ross must've been in the kitchen with Brigitte and Mary because she wasn't in the room. The men all stood at the bar. Ted Brock was behind it, mixing drinks. Enid Harrell sat in a chair and watched Phyllis's anguish, no expression on her own face. She just kept staring at the devastation and pain that was playing out before her eyes. In that moment, I wanted to go up to the doctor's wife and slug her. She was a social nitwit. I didn't like her in the least. Mrs. Brock stood looking out the window, waiting for the ambulance to arrive. When it did, she went to the door.

Three men in suits entered. Accompanying them were two ambulance attendants and one police officer in uniform. Mrs. Brock gestured to the room Eddie Killburn was in. All of them, except one, went immediately to where the body was. One stayed behind for a moment.

"I'm Detective Kotarski. I suppose I don't have to tell you people not to leave until we've had a chance to talk to you. Just stay put and we'll get to you in a bit."

Mary entered the room carrying a tray with several cups on it filled with coffee. Lillian Ross was behind her. The women all reached for one, except for Phyllis. The men were sipping their drinks at the bar. No one was talking. I grabbed a cup of the coffee and took mine back to the kitchen. I sat at the table across from a swollen eyed Brigitte and next to Mary.

"You going to be okay?" I asked Brigitte.

She nodded and her tears started to flow again. She laid her head down on her arm, which was resting on the table.

"What happened in there, Mr. Flanagan?" Mary asked.

"I don't know," I shrugged and shook my head.

"But he's so young…" Her voice trailed off.

We sat in silence, looking down at the table. As the moments passed, it seemed like hours. Occasionally, I could hear mutterings from where the others were, but mainly, they, too, were quiet. Time ticked away and the two women and I just looked past each other and said nothing. It was about twenty-five minutes later when I heard a commotion coming from the other room and rose to see what was going on. Phyllis was being restrained by

Dr. Harrell as the ambulance attendants carried the still body of her husband out of the house on a stretcher. She was crying "No! No!" as they passed through the front door with him. It was a heart wrenching sight. One of the men in a suit followed them out. I assumed this was the medical examiner. He was a man of medium height and had gray hair worn in a very short military cut. He stopped just outside the door and turned back to the two detectives.

"I'll let you know more after I've done some testing."

Kotarski said, "Thanks, Jim," and then he shut the front door.

One by one the two detectives called us into the kitchen. They had talked to Brigitte and Mary first and allowed them to retreat to their quarters. By the time I was summoned to the kitchen table, it was well after midnight. Kotarski reintroduced himself and introduced his partner as Detective Walsh.

"Have a seat, Mr. uh—"

"Flanagan," I said.

"Okay, Mr. Flanagan. We need you to think back over the evening and let us know if you noticed if Mr. Killburn was feeling ill at any time, or if you noticed anything at all out of the ordinary."

Detective Kotarski was asking the questions and Detective Walsh was taking the notes. I told them exactly who I was and why I'd been in attendance tonight. There was nothing out of the ordinary that I'd noticed. I'd learned long ago to be straight with the police. It didn't pay to fabricate anything or to hide any information— they always found it out in the end. The questioning was brief. As they had with the others, they took the address and phone number of where I was staying before they let me go.

Detective Walsh moved to Mary's door and knocked softly on it. She opened it, dressed in her nightgown and robe, her eyes red and watery.

"You might want to help Mrs. Killburn up to her room and get her settled in," he said.

She nodded and moved through the kitchen, but stopped when she saw me standing by the table.

"Oh, Mr. Flanagan," she said in a weak and jittery voice. Then she moved closer, laying her head on my chest and putting her arms around my waist. I gave her a hug.

"Stay strong, Mary," I said. "I'll be in touch."

She backed away and went to her employer.

****

It was 1:17 a.m. when I pulled up in the drive at Harry's house. I parked the car in the garage and entered through the back door. It was dark inside and I snapped on the kitchen light. I removed my coat and hat and heard something rustle. Checking my coat pocket, I found the bag of coffee Mary had put there earlier this evening, and I placed it on the counter. Throwing my coat over one chair at the table, I pulled out another and sat in it. Somehow, I couldn't quite believe that Eddie Killburn was dead. What the hell had happened to him? He was fine one minute, playing the piano and singing. The next minute he was dead. I replayed all the events of the evening and I couldn't recall him saying he felt ill, or a time when he looked to be not feeling well. He seemed in good spirits throughout the entire event. If it *had* been foul play, who could've done this? *What* could they have done? I tried to think back to when I was sitting on the couch. Captain Charles Ross and his wife had joined me and while talking, I'd seen Dabney Harrell enter the room Eddie was in. But I'd seen him come out and Eddie had obviously started to play again because I'd heard him. Then I saw Major Ted Brock go to Eddie. Had Eddie resumed playing after his talk with the major? I racked my brain trying to recall. It was no use; I was too tired to think clearly.

I looked up and saw Harry standing in the doorway of the kitchen. He yawned.

"Hey, Sam," he said. "So, how was the party?"

"You're not going to believe this," I answered.

I told him about the entire evening, from start to finish. He stared at me and never interrupted. When I was done with my story, he gave a low whistle.

"Wow, what a hell of a party," he said.

"Yeah, and what a hell of a story for the Trib, huh?" I responded.

Judith White

CHAPTER EIGHTEEN

One would've thought I would not have been able to sleep easily that night, but I did. As soon as my head hit the pillow, I was out like a log. If trains and nightmares tried to sabotage my sleep, they didn't succeed. I slept a whole nine hours, waking at 11:30 a.m. After rising from bed and dressing, I still felt as though I was in a bad dream. Eddie Killburn was alive and well and had the promise of youth on his side up until last night. Now he would forever be only a memory.

Myra was polishing the coffee table in the living room. She was on her knees with her back to me. Instead of entering the room, I went in the opposite direction to the kitchen. There I found the coffee pot sitting on an unlit burner on the stove. I put my fingers to it and found it was still hot. Grabbing a cup from the cupboard, I filled it with the black beverage, and took a seat at the kitchen table. Myra was listening to a Sunday sermon by Pastor Billy Tuggs, a Baptist radio preacher broadcasting from St. Louis, Missouri. His words drifted to where I sat.

"…remind you once again that James says, 'We *sin* when we leave God out of our plans and purposes.' John states that *all* unrighteous thoughts, words, and actions are *sin*. Our brother in Christ, Paul, declares that we *sin* when we compromise our own conscience, and John says we *sin* when we transgress the law of the Almighty God. And just what is the consequence of this *sin* and all others, brothers and sisters? *For the wages of sin is death*!" he yelled.

My mind returned to Eddie. What was his terrible sin? Was it the sin of getting involved with another woman while he was married? What made his sin any different than the rest of ours that his life would be taken at such an early age? Why was his punishment such a harsh punishment? Was this God's judgment upon him because of his indiscretion? I didn't believe that anymore than I believed in the tooth fairy.

The radio went silent and I heard Myra moving toward the kitchen.

"Ah, you're up," she said when she saw me. "I can fix you some breakfast if you'd like."

"No, but thanks. I guess I'm not very hungry this morning."

"Harry told me what happened last night," she said. "He called 'bout an hour ago and wants you to call him back as soon as you can. We skipped church and he went into work to see if he could find anything out. I'm so sorry, Sam. I know he was a friend."

"Did anyone else call for me?" I asked.

I was expecting Phyllis to call or maybe even the detectives from last night. But I was disappointed to hear there had been no other calls. And then I thought about what Myra had just said. I *know he was a friend.* Eddie wasn't a friend. I hardly knew him. So, why was I consumed with sadness and injustice? Maybe, deep down, I thought he was the type that *could've* become a friend. Even though he was supposed to be the 'bad guy' in taking up with Corinne Schneider, maybe I couldn't help but see him as he presented himself to me; as the good guy.

I rose from the table and moved to the phone. Myra opened her personal directory and pointed to the number of Harry's work. I dialed and waited through five rings.

"Hello, Chicago Tribune. How may I help you?" a female voice answered.

"I'd like to speak to Harry Blevins. He's a reporter."

"Hold on while I connect you."

Almost a full two minutes passed before Harry's voice sounded in my ear.

"Chicago Tribune. This is Harry Blevins speaking."

"Harry, it's Sam," I told him.

"Oh Sam, glad you called. Listen, I've been trying to get some information about last night. And, believe me, it's not been easy to get. I talked to Detective Herb Walsh a couple of times this morning and—"

I interrupted him.

"Did you say Detective Walsh? He was one of the guys at the estate last night."

"Yeah? He's a good guy—feeds me information I shouldn't have sometimes. We've become somewhat friends over the years. Anyway, he says this one is going to get brushed under the carpet. They are going to lay real low on this one and he won't tell me why. Well, he won't tell me *yet*. He usually comes through if I promise to play it right and not be a big mouth."

My pulse started to quicken and I felt my blood pressure rise. I was silent, wondering what it all meant. I was afraid to even admit that it meant Eddie didn't die of natural causes.

"Sam? You still with me?" Harry asked.

"Yeah, yeah; just thinking that this obviously means—"

"Right!" Harry cut in. "There's something fishy about his death. That was no heart attack, my friend!"

****

Okay, if it wasn't a heart attack, if it was murder, why brush it under the carpet? Why keep quiet about it, *especially* if it was murder? I didn't get it. Before I returned to my coffee, I dialed the Killburn residence; maybe Phyllis knew more about this than I did. I had to see if she'd heard anything. Mary answered the phone, not sounding her usual self.

"Hello, Mary. How are things there?"

"Oh, Mr. Flanagan; it feels as if we're livin' a nightmare here."

I heard her begin to weep softly.

"I know, Mary, I know. How is Phyllis doing? Is she around?"

"She's up in her room. She's already instructed us she wants to see no one and wants to talk to no one. I'm sorry, Mr. Flanagan. Those two detectives came here early this mornin' and talked to her. After they left, she told us not to bother her and she's been locked away ever since. I don't think the poor darlin' is doin' too well. When I see her, I can tell her that ya called."

"That's fine. Tell her, too, that I'd like her to call me back as soon as she can."

I gave her Harry and Myra's number and we disconnected.

****

Harry didn't make it home until way past dinnertime. He was holed up with other reporters at the Chicago police station, trying to get whatever information he could. He got nothing additional to the little leak he'd received this morning. No call came from the Whitaker estate, so I tried again to contact Phyllis at 9:30 at night and then again at 10:15. There was no answer either time. I finally gave up and went to bed, filled with anxiety.

Judith White

CHAPTER NINETEEN

"Sam, she's on the phone. Hurry up!"

I jumped. Myra had her head just inside the bedroom door. I rolled over and looked at the clock. It was barely 7:30 on Monday morning. She backed out of the room when she knew I wasn't about to roll over and go back to sleep. When she was gone I leapt out of bed, hopping into my pants. I grabbed my shirt and slipped my arms through it without fastening the buttons. Entering the kitchen, I grabbed the receiver, which was sitting on the counter near the sink.

"Hello?" I said, a bit out of breath.

"Mr. Flanagan, I woke you, didn't I?"

"Don't worry about that. And please, call me Sam. How are you doing, Phyllis? I tried to get hold of you a few times yesterday. Are you alright?"

"No, I'm a wreck. I can't sleep, I haven't eaten; I feel like a zombie. I don't know what's going on, and I don't know what happened. Do you know what that feels like? To know half of your life has died and you don't know why?"

She became quiet and I had a hard time finding words to comfort her.

"No, I don't know what that's like," was all I could think of to say.

"I called you for a specific reason, Sam. The police chief called almost a half hour ago and wants to see me at the station. He said it's important. I think he may have some news for me, but I don't want to go in there alone. I want you to go with me, if you're willing."

"What time does he want to see you?" I asked.

"He told me anywhere between 9:00 and 9:30," she said in a flat voice.

"I'll be there by 9:00," I told her. "Would you like me to swing by and pick you up?"

"No, Augie will drive me. I have to make arrangements for the funeral afterwards." She paused and I could only hear shallow breathing. Then she said, "Sam? I don't know what I'm going to do without him. I loved him so much."

"I know you did."

But I was talking into a dead connection. She'd already hung up.

In the last thirty six hours, I'd learned just how much Phyllis really *did* love him. Before his death, she hadn't shown this much depth, but there was no mistaking her emotion now. The woman was very much in pain.

****

It was ten minutes to nine o'clock when I arrived on Racine Avenue and parked across from the police station. I got out of the car and crossed the street, but I didn't enter the building. Instead, I pulled out a cigarette and lit it. Walking back and forth in front of the entrance, I waited for Phyllis's arrival. I was nervous and anxious, wondering what the chief's news would be. The sun was shining bright and whatever snow fell on Saturday night, it hadn't stuck to the ground. There were just remnants of the white flakes on the streets and walkways. The wind was tamer today than it had been since I'd arrived in Chicago. The temperature must've been close to forty. I smoked my cigarette and discarded the butt on the sidewalk, then immediately lit another. I'd taken maybe three hits on it when I spied the Super Deluxe approaching on Racine. I dropped the smoke and stamped it out with my shoe.

The car pulled into the parking lot at the station and I waited for them to come around front. Augie immediately crossed the street and went into a restaurant called *Uncle Pete's*. No doubt he would be eying the front of the station house to see when Phyllis had finished her business and was ready to leave. I opened the door and Phyllis entered ahead of me. We said nothing to each other. I couldn't help but notice her eyes were puffy and she looked worn out. We were shown to the office of the chief of police, but I didn't fail to notice the stares as we passed the other officers and detectives. Somehow, I got the feeling that they didn't know I would be accompanying Phyllis, and it was obvious they didn't approve of my presence.

The man who stood behind the desk in the office was probably six feet tall. He had a good thirty pounds on me, but he was solidly built and appeared to be in good shape. His hair was salt and pepper and he had a nose

175

that was a little too large for his face, which was pock marked. The man's ears stuck out further than normal from his head and, as God is my witness, he didn't have a right ear lobe. It gave him the appearance of being off balance. His eyes were dark brown and when he saw me, his face turned to stone. Phyllis immediately went to him and he hugged her. These two knew each other; that much was evident.

"Oh, Michael," she said as she rested in his arms.

"I'm so sorry, Phyllis," he said in an Irish brogue.

She pulled away from him and nodded, looking down at the floor. He looked past her and stared at me and finally gestured toward me.

"Who's he? This should really be private."

"Oh, forgive me," she said. "This is Sam Flanagan, the detective I told your men I'd hired. Sam, this is Police Chief Michael O'Bannon. I want him here, Michael."

I stepped forward and extended my hand, but the man turned away from me and sat behind his desk without shaking it. Saying nothing, I turned and sat in one of the two chairs he had across from him. Phyllis sat down in the other. He looked at me with cold eyes.

"I don't know why you need to be included in this. Your job is done; you have no part in this. So let's get this straight—you'll keep your mouth shut."

"Let's get *this* straight," I told him, giving him a stare that matched his. "The lady asked me to accompany her and that's why I'm here. I happened to be there when we ended up with a dead body on our hands and I'd like to know why."

"What did you say your name was again?" he asked me.

"I didn't say. The lady told you it was Flanagan. Sam Flanagan."

"It figures."

He slapped his desk with the palm of his open hand and then wagged a thick forefinger at me.

"I suppose you're one of the rotten Wexford Flanagan's!"

I remembered Mary had mentioned this, too. *What in the hell was up with the Flanagan family from Wexford?* I thought. I rubbed my temple and allowed an exaggerated sigh to escape my lips.

"My family comes from Tralee, Chief."

"Yeah? Well if I find out you're lying to me—"

Phyllis interrupted him with the pounding of her fist on his desk.

"Michael!" she yelled. "I don't have time for this and I don't have the strength. What did you want to see me about? I've told your men all I know. I have things to arrange!"

And then she started to cry. She removed a handkerchief from her purse and held it to her eyes as if it were a cold compress, and sighed heavily. The chief turned his gaze toward her, and he wore an expression of guilt. He picked up his phone and dialed.

"Get Kotarski and Walsh in here and see if you can find Doc Powell. I want him in here, too."

He replaced the receiver, leaned back in his chair and muttered a half-audible apology to Phyllis. I smiled inwardly, enjoying his discomfort.

Five minutes later, Detectives Kotarski and Walsh had joined us, along with Dr. Jim Powell. When we were all assembled, O'Bannon rolled his chair out from behind his desk and moved closer to Phyllis. He leaned in with his elbows on his knees.

"Now, I'm going to tell you what we think happened on the night of your dinner party. You hired this guy," he indicated me with a tilt of his head, "because you suspected your husband of seeing another woman. You said Eddie had threatened you, right?"

"Yes," Phyllis said, hesitantly.

He looked over at me and I confirmed his statement with a slight nod.

"You told Walt and Herb here that, after you'd all eaten dinner, you'd had a drink and were mixing yourself another when Mr. Flanagan here hit you with the news of this other woman, right? You were standing by the bar at the time, but after this shock, you left what you were doing and you wanted to go upstairs. At that time, your husband came up to you and saw your empty glass and offered to make you another drink. He took your glass to refill it, right?"

Phyllis nodded.

I creased my forehead and thought back to the night of the party. This was all new to me. I hadn't seen Eddie approach Phyllis. Why hadn't I seen him? It finally dawned on me that after talking to Phyllis that night while standing at the bar, I'd gone into the kitchen to get more coffee and stayed there for a bit, talking to Mary.

He continued. "He handed you the drink; and you told the detectives that Eddie then went into the next room to play the piano."

"Yes," Phyllis said.

"And then what did you do?" he asked her.

Kotarski and Walsh were standing by the window, their eyes focused on Phyllis. Dr. Powell sat on the edge of O'Bannon's desk, his right leg swinging. Phyllis's chest heaved with her intake of breath.

"I was torn between going up to my room, getting away from everyone for a few minutes, or having it out with him. I followed Eddie into the room. I was going to ask him about this woman, this nurse, and then I thought better of it. We had a house full of people, for goodness sake. He was playing at the piano and when I saw him I thought I was going to lose it, so I remember turning toward the fireplace. I didn't want him to see any tears. Once I got hold of myself, I went up to him and told him I would be upstairs for a few moments, just so he would know where I was at and wouldn't come looking for me, I guess. I don't even think he'd noticed I was in the room with him until I actually went up to him. But, Michael, what does this have to do with anything?"

"And you didn't take a sip of that drink or take that drink with you upstairs?" O'Bannon asked.

"Oh...I don't know *what* I did with it. I don't *know* if I took a sip. I wasn't thinking clearly. I just wanted to get away from the crowd for a few moments to gather my composure." She became frustrated. "Oh, what does this have to *do* with anything? What are you *getting* at? I don't understand! So *what*? I *didn't take the stupid drink with me!*"

O'Bannon looked at the medical examiner and he took over.

"Mrs. Killburn, we think that you left that drink behind, possibly on the fireplace mantle? We aren't sure anymore than you are. But we believe when your husband went to sit on the couch, he saw it and maybe mistook it for his own. He grabbed it and sat down and drank it."

I was getting their implications before Phyllis was, and what they were implying sent a chill running through me.

"Okay," she said. "So what?"

The doctor continued. "We tested the martini glass we'd bagged, which was found on the floor under your husband's hand. There was also one olive lying on the floor next to the glass. We tested that and your husband's blood. All three things contained methyl alcohol, a very toxic substance. We think that was the drink he made for you, and you left it behind. He mistakenly drank it."

Phyllis stiffened.

"How can you be sure it was my glass? You can't be sure of that."

"No, we can't be sure," Kotarski spoke up. "But unless your husband wore a shade of rose lipstick Saturday night, we figure it was yours. There were very faint traces of lipstick on the outer rim of the martini glass. He probably didn't notice it when he drank his own poison."

Her eyes grew wide.

"That's why this should've been private," the chief said to Phyllis, while staring at me. "We're sure you wouldn't want this information to get out and be spread around town."

Judith White

CHAPTER TWENTY

Uncle Pete's wasn't busy. An elderly couple sat at a table near the window and three uniformed police officers were sitting on stools at the counter, drinking coffee. It was only a few minutes after eleven o'clock, but I didn't want to return to the house. After our meeting in Chief Michael O'Bannon's office, I needed to be alone with my thoughts.

Upon hearing the news that her husband had tried to kill her, the only words to come out of Phyllis's mouth were, "He tried to poison me? I don't believe it!" I couldn't quite believe it, either. *The poor fool. He drank his own concoction*, I thought. Life is full of mistakes, and the best we can hope for is to learn from them and then carry on until we make the next one. But when we make a mistake as grave as the one Eddie had made, we never get the chance to start over and go in a different direction. There's only one thing that is permanent in life, and that is there's an end to it; there is death awaiting us. From our birth until the day of our departure, we hold all the cards in deciding our fate. Eddie made the wrong decision and it had cost him dearly. The consequences for him were as permanent as it would ever get. In choosing his course of action, Eddie altered the lives of many others. I thought about not only Phyllis, but Turk and Ginny at the *Easy Street Lounge*, as well. They'd lost a friend. And what about Lou? Lou would never hear the sweet sound of Eddie's music ever again. I thought of Corinne Schneider. Had she heard the news? How would she react? No doubt when she heard of her loss, she'd have to do her suffering alone and in silence. He wouldn't be there to hold her and pat her on the back. There would never be another time that she would lay her head against his shoulder. He would never be able to comfort her ever again. She, like Phyllis, was alone in this world now.

The waitress arrived with my pea soup and glass of milk. I crumbled crackers in the bowl and began to eat, not really tasting it. After I'd finished with it, I didn't want to leave so I ordered a piece of lemon meringue pie. Three bites into it, I shoved it away from me. It was too sour. I pulled out a cigarette and smoked it. My job in Chicago was over. The case was finished. It had a bad ending and I somehow felt a complicity in its outcome. I didn't know why.

****

Later that evening at Harry and Myra's, I packed the little I had brought with me to Chicago. Tomorrow at ten in the morning, a Greyhound bus was leaving for Detroit and I would be on it. Dialing the Killburn residence, I got no answer. I had wanted to say goodbye to Phyllis, but especially to Mary. I'd never been good at saying farewell to people whom I liked, and I liked Mary Alice Mullane a lot.

Harry had returned home from work after dinner. He found me alone in the living room sitting in the chair and smoking a cigarette.

"Hey, what information did you get out of O'Bannon's office?" he asked me.

"Information that is too hard to believe," I said, torn between whether I should tell him or not.

It didn't feel right withholding this from Harry, but he was a reporter and I knew he'd want to make good on a story about all the sordid details.

"Yeah, well I imagine you found out the same thing I did," he said. "I talked to Herb Walsh again today. Of course, I'm sworn to secrecy, but I *am* going to do a human interest piece. You know, on Eddie. I guess they're going to play it like they can't seem to find a cause of death, it's baffled them. Could've been hereditary or a heart defect at birth; no foul play involved—that kind of thing. They want to protect her from the humiliation at all costs." He shook his head. "What an idiot!" he said.

I bristled at his last statement and looked at him.

"I know," he said. "I can't quite think of Eddie Killburn as being that idiotic, either. He wasn't the devious type, or so I thought. This whole thing has me baffled. I can't imagine him even thinking of something like this. I would never have thought he had it in him. It wasn't like him."

I agreed. It wasn't like him and I didn't even *know* him, but he'd impressed me in a whole other way.

185

I told Harry of my plans for leaving and he expressed a bit of regret, saying he and Myra would miss me. I'd miss them, too, but I'd been here almost two weeks. I never thought I would be here this long. It was time for me to get home to my grandmother.

****

Harry drove me to the station and Myra insisted on coming along. I hated saying goodbye to them, but I was eager to get home and settled into my normal routine. Something had bothered me ever since arriving here, and with Eddie's death, the importance of saying it was foremost in my mind. We don't always have the luxury of time on our side, and I thought I would talk to my friend while I had the opportunity. Myra was sitting on a bench in the terminal and I took Harry aside.

"When I first arrived here, Myra had a bruise on her cheek," I began.

Harry's face seemed to drain of color. I suddenly felt very awkward, but I pushed myself to continue.

"I love you like a brother, Harry, but so help me God, if I ever hear of you—"

He cut me off by holding up a hand.

"Enough said. You won't. Not ever!"

We left it at that.

Finally, people were boarding the bus to Detroit. I hugged Harry and shook his hand. I hugged Myra and gently kissed her on the cheek. I thanked them for all the hospitality they had shown me, and I didn't feel that I adequately communicated how deeply grateful I really felt. Hopefully, the ten dollars in the envelope I had left laying on the bed I had slept in for the past almost two weeks would help to reinforce my appreciation. I stepped onto the bus and left Chicago and the Killburn case behind.

Judith White

CHAPTER TWENTY ONE

The bus rolled into Detroit at 6:10 p.m., twenty-five minutes later than its estimated time of arrival. I unlocked the '38 Chevy and tried to shake off a feeling of sadness. Not only had I left behind people that I didn't want to leave behind, but I felt something had been left incomplete in Chicago. I didn't know what that something was.

The Chevy didn't start when I turned the key. I pumped the accelerator a few times, turned the key again, and the engine sputtered, but still didn't catch. After two more tries, I gave up. I retraced my steps and entered the bus terminal once again. Two of the five pay phones were available and I went to one and looked up the number of the service station I was used to dealing with. At this hour, I didn't think anyone would be there, but it wouldn't hurt to try. I was surprised when my call was answered.

"Martin's Filling Station and Auto Service."

"Hep, is that you? It's Sam Flanagan."

"Hey, Sam! You're lucky. I was just about to walk out for the day. What can I do for you?"

"Eh, the Chevy won't start. I got it parked in the lot of the Greyhound station. If you're heading home, you can always take care of this tomorrow. But I want you to tow it in and have a look at it. A couple of weeks ago, I heard a noise under the hood."

"Nah, might as well do it now and get it over with. You're at the bus station, you say? You going somewhere?"

"I been somewhere. Just got in about twenty minutes ago."

"Well, stay put. I'll head on over and I can give you a ride home."

Hep Cat Martin was a man in his mid-forties who'd been married to the same woman since he was seventeen. He and Irma had nine children and a house full of animals: three dogs, four cats and a hamster. The man had been given the nickname of Hep Cat when he'd formed a neighborhood band that practiced out in his garage when he wasn't running his filling station and auto repair shop. His instrument was the saxophone and he wasn't half-bad at playing it. The couple of songs that he had written were pretty jive. Everyone called him Hep or Hep Cat nowadays, and I found it puzzling that I couldn't recall what his actual given name was at the moment. Over the years he'd built his business by being an excellent mechanic and by being fair and reasonable with his prices. He was a good man.

I'd been standing inside the bus terminal, watching out the huge front window for his arrival. He pulled up to the Chevy and I walked out to greet him. He nodded toward the truck.

"Get in," he said. "No sense for the *two* of us to freeze our rears off."

I sat in the passenger side amongst the litter on the front seat and floor. He lifted the hood of my car and buried his head under it for some minutes. He finally emerged, wiped his hands down the sides of his overalls, and slammed the hood shut. After he hooked up the Chevy, he got in, started the engine, and began pulling out.

"You'll have to apologize for me to Irma for making you late tonight," I said.

"Shoot, Sam; she's used to this. Seems this winter is playing havoc with everyone's transportation. We've been busy at the shop."

"How's the family doing?" I asked him.

He looked over at me, bobbing his head up and down.

"Good. They're all doing good." He started to laugh. "My kid, Jimmy, been bringing home bad grades all year this year. I sat him down and told him for every A he gets on this next card; I'll fork over a dime. Well, the little shit brought home this next report card and he's got six A's on it. I *knew* he was just being lazy. Now I gotta come up with a way to hand over sixty cents. And if he ever lets on about this to the others, I'll have one hell of a mess on my hands."

"Which one is Jimmy?"

"He's my nine year old."

****

The house on St. Aubin Street was dark. Either my grandmother was out, which was unlikely, or she was dozing. I found the front door unlocked. As soon as I entered, I heard the radio blaring with an episode of *The Inner Sanctum*. Feeling my way toward the dining room, I found the floor model wireless and shut it off. I turned on the lamp, which was on a table to its right. Turning around, I saw Gran.

She was slumped over the right arm of her wooden rocking chair, her hand pointing to the floor. Her chin was forward, resting on her chest. A vision of Eddie Killburn flashed through my mind. O*h dear God, Ruby*, I thought. My eyes filled with moisture and I just stood there looking at her for a full half minute. She needed me in her last moments on earth and I hadn't been here for her. What would I do without her? I moved slowly to where she was. I bent down and placed my fingertips on her dangling wrist. She was still warm. Suddenly, she jumped and straightened, wide eyed, in her chair. She let out a loud snort and I jumped back in fear, letting out a scream as I did so. I put my hand on my chest, trying to recapture my breath.

"For God's sake," I said. "I thought you were dead! You scared the hell out of me!"

She looked up at me and belched loudly.

"Oh my goodness!" she uttered. "That beer wasn't bad." And then she asked, "Am I?"

"Are you *what*?" I asked.

"Am I dead?"

"Oh, you're impossible," I said, heading toward the kitchen and snapping the light on. "Would you be talking to me if you were dead? No, you're not dead, Gran."

She followed me into the room.

"Well, you might be dead, too," she reasoned. "*Then* I'd be talking to you."

"Don't think that couldn't happen. You're going to give me a heart attack one of these days!"

"Good thing I'm not, though. Your grandfather would be mighty upset to see I'd been drinking beer."

As far as I had known, Ruby Flanagan had never had a drop of alcohol in her life. She'd argued with my grandfather for years over his indulging in whiskey. It shocked me that she'd gotten drunk while drinking beer this afternoon. I asked her about the beer and she told me her friend, Helen, had come over and brought it with her. Sunday, they had attended church, where Pastor Benjamin Farron had railed against the sin of imbibing. This got Helen to thinking, and she'd come over to Ruby's about noon, bringing six bottles of beer with her. She told her friend that they'd never committed any of the sins which the pastor had been preaching about; the sins of drinking alcohol, cursing and fornication, and it was high time they found out about this fascination with drinking.

"We each drank half a bottle of beer, and then Helen said we should each say a swear word. I chose damn and Helen yelled out bastard real loud, just like she was really calling someone that. You shoulda heard her, Sam. She was real convincing."

Rolling my eyes toward the ceiling, I opened the icebox and looked inside. There wasn't much there. I pulled out the eggs and the pound of bacon. I'd make dinner for us. Gran needed some food in her stomach. She continued telling me about Helen's visit.

"Helen took another couple of swigs and all of a sudden she jumped up from her chair and ran toward the bathroom. I guess it didn't sit well on her stomach, 'cause she was in there throwin' up. She came out and said she'd wet her drawers while she was regurgitatin', so she left right away. But I finished my beer and drank two more."

I turned from the stove to face my grandmother, who was sitting at the kitchen table.

"You drank *three* beers?" I asked. "No wonder you passed out. Didn't Albie show up today?"

She shrugged. "If he did, I didn't hear him knock at the door."

No, I guess she wouldn't have.

****

It was late Wednesday night when I got a call from Hep Martin. He didn't have good news.

"I hate to tell you this, buddy, but you've spun a rod bearing. It's gonna take some work and money to get her going again. I'll see what I can do to ease the pain of the cost."

I looked toward heaven and said, "What else?" and then sighed.

Hep mistook my words for being aimed at him.

"Nothing else that I can see. You want me to go ahead with fixing her up?"

What else could I do? I gave him the green light on starting the repairs.

I went into the office on Thursday; I had to pay for a taxicab to get me there. There was a note attached to the outside of my door. I grabbed it and went inside. It was from a Mr. Reuven Rosenfeld, asking me to call him at his place of business. I dialed the number, and a feminine voice answered.

"Rosenfeld Jeweler's."

"I'd like to talk to Mr. Rosenfeld, please," I said.

"Which one, sir; David or his father, Reuven?"

"Reuven," I clarified.

He was on the phone within seconds. He was relieved when he'd found out who was calling him.

"Oh, Mr. Flanagan, I'm so glad you called me. I have a problem I need looking into. I've had some bad luck at having some items go missing. At least once a week lately, I've opened the store to find something else gone. I want you to find who's doing this so I can put a stop to it."

"Have you contacted the police? You should probably start with them first," I suggested.

"I don't want to do that. I'm very much afraid it's an inside job, and I'd rather deal with it in my own way, depending on who the culprit is, if that's the case."

Agreeing to take on the assignment, I told him I didn't have access to an automobile at the moment, and might not have transportation for another couple of days. He told me just to get to it as soon as possible. I wrote down the address of the jeweler's and hung up.

I was cleaning out my file cabinet, tossing out old case files, when my phone rang. It was about 2:00 in the afternoon.

"Flanagan Investigations," I said into the receiver.

"Mr. Flanagan, this is June McKenna. How are you?"

I was very pleasantly surprised at hearing her voice.

"June! Well, *this* is a surprise. I'm fine, how are you?"

And then a thought loomed large in my mind, and I stiffened with apprehension.

"Nothing's happened to Myra, has it?"

"No, no, she's fine. Her and Harry came over for dinner last night. I read Harry's piece in the Tribune about Eddie Killburn. It's an excellent story, but it says they don't know how he died. I asked Harry about it last night, but he claims to know nothing. I've come to know Harry pretty well, Mr. Flanagan, and I think he's lying. I think he knows and I bet you do, too."

"I don't know anything, June. What's the sudden interest in Eddie all about?"

"I'm mainly calling for a very good friend who is quite distraught. She deserves to know what happened."

"Are you talking about Corinne Schneider?" I asked. I suddenly felt myself getting angry. "Because if you are, he also has a wife who is very distraught, too. And she deserved a hell of a lot more!"

There was nothing but silence on the other end of the phone. Had she hung up?

"Are you there?" I asked.

"Yes," she said in a faint whisper.

And then she found her voice and came back stronger than ever.

"Just what are you getting at, Mr. Flanagan? I'd like to know!"

"What I'm getting at is the difference between right and wrong! The man had a wife, and I've got to side with *her* on this one. *She* has my sympathy! Your *friend* may have loved him, too, but she was the *other woman* and it was *her* choice to be that."

I ran out of words and grew silent. What she said next stung.

"You are more stupid than I could've ever imagined you being! You are truly ignorant! Corinne wasn't *the other woman*, as you put it! She had no such relationship with Eddie Killburn! How could you even *think* that?"

I stared straight ahead and felt an electricity shoot through my body. I sat straighter in my chair. Just what the hell was going on here?

"I think we'd better start over," I said, weakly.

Judith White

CHAPTER TWENTY TWO

The story went something like this. Corinne had married Artie Schneider at the tender age of nineteen, five years ago. She'd been in training to become a nurse when she'd met him. With the outbreak of the war, Artie joined the United States Navy in January of 1942. His ship was present during the fighting at the Battle of Guadalcanal, which was still raging. His vessel had gotten hit by the Japanese in early November, 1942. It hadn't been completely destroyed, but several of the seamen had either been killed or wounded. Artie was lucky in that he hadn't lost his life, but he wasn't so lucky in that he'd lost his eyesight and his right leg, just above the knee. He'd been transported home in mid-November of last year, and had been in the *Edward Hines, Jr. Memorial Hospital* ever since. Corinne had been an eyewitness account to the work that Eddie Killburn had been doing with other wounded soldiers; all of the medical staff had seen the benefit of Eddie working with the vets, including June. He was at the hospital at least four days out of a seven-day period, sometimes more. Corinne had told Eddie of her husband's case and asked for his help. The volunteer work that Eddie Killburn had performed for the U.S. military included counseling and providing assistance with therapy whenever he was allowed. After all, he'd been in the position himself back in 1940 with the injury to his own leg. He knew how they felt, and could empathize and sympathize with them. The young man filled them with encouragement and the will to go on living when they just felt like giving up. Eddie took one of the large rooms at the hospital that was being used for storage and brought in a crew to move the equipment out and to help him in transforming the area into a small recreational facility for the battered soldiers. They gathered there to listen to the radio or play games of checkers and cards. The room was used as a visitation area when family and friends came to see them. The soldiers could come there to commiserate or just show up to listen to Eddie play for them on the new upright piano he'd purchased. The piano was community property, he'd told them, and they, too, played songs and sang along with the others.

Artie Schneider's case was particularly difficult. He'd begged the medical staff to end his suffering. He shared his suicidal thoughts with Eddie. Corinne had been included in the counseling of her husband, whom she dearly loved and didn't want to release to death. Eddie referred to Corinne as 'the rock' around the hospital because of her stoicism.

I thought back to the conversation between Eddie and Dr. Dabney Harrell on the night of the party, almost a week ago now. Eddie's words sounded in my ears again. *She's the stronger of the two...there's just something about Corinne....* Corinne was the stronger of the two between her husband and herself! It had nothing to do with Phyllis! *She's going to be of so much support....* Corinne was going to be of so much support to her husband, not to Eddie! And what was the time bomb Dr. Harrell had spoken of? Might it be that he meant he was concerned that Corinne was taking on too much emotionally? Could it be that he thought the young woman might crack under the enormous pressure at some point? It all made perfect sense.

"So you see, Mr. Flanagan," June said. "Corinne loved Eddie very much, as we all did here. But she was, and still is, very much in love with her husband. The day Eddie Killburn died was one that affected every staff member here, as well as every patient. I don't know what those men will do without him."

I leaned back in my chair and looked down, realizing I'd been more than an idiot in jumping to conclusions on this case. Embarrassment and shame engulfed me. My apology to June was conveyed in the strongest of possible terms and I prayed she could feel the sincerity of my sorrow. I told her I didn't have all the facts, but when I had them, she'd be one of the first to know what had happened. What I *didn't* tell her was what was said in O'Bannon's office, though. More investigation was needed on this before she became aware of what that conversation was all about.

Throwing all my old files back into the cabinet, I grabbed for my coat and hat. I left the office, locking up for the day. Surely I'd find a cab cruising down, or parked on, Woodward Avenue to take me home. I was calling it quits for the day.

****

When the taxi pulled up to the house, I saw Helen's new vehicle sitting in the drive. Her husband had died two years earlier, leaving her enough money to purchase it, along with the funds to see her through her remaining years. When I walked in, they were seated in the living room. They became very quiet when I entered. I looked from one to the other, wondering what they were up to. Helen was sitting in a chair with a glass of orange juice on the end table beside her. My grandmother was on the sofa. Again, there was a glass of the juice on the table. Both glasses contained ice, which I thought was strange. I'd never known my grandmother to add ice to juice. They caught me looking from one to the other and my grandmother spoke.

"It's only juice, dear. Don't go throwing a conniption."

Moving through the room on my way to the kitchen, I passed Helen, and spied the very top of a bottle of vodka sticking out of her purse. I pretended I didn't see it, and their eyes followed me until I was out of sight. Almost immediately I could hear their silence being broken by soft snickering. I glanced at my watch. It was 3:30 in the afternoon. Moving to the icebox, I peered inside. What could I throw together for dinner? No doubt we'd be having Helen as our guest. And then I thought about how glad I was that there were clean sheets on my bed. Somehow, I knew I'd have to give up my sleeping spot for my grandmother's friend for a night, while I slept on the couch.

****

I sat in Helen's car a block down from *Rosenfeld Jeweler's* on Gratiot Avenue. I was watching the front entrance of the business. It was a quarter after nine. At dinner, I'd asked Helen if I could use the car, and she agreed and then started giggling. I admit I'd taken advantage of the situation. I made both of them change into nightgowns after they'd eaten. Helen wore one of my grandmother's and it was three sizes too big for her. They both wanted to sleep in Gran's double bed and leave the door to the room wide open with the radio on. The radio was located in the dining room and Gran's bedroom door opened onto it. They didn't want to miss tonight's episode of *Fibber McGee and Molly*. Both were giddy with excitement at having a sleep over like the young girls did nowadays. Before I left the house for my night of surveillance, I went to where Helen's purse was sitting and removed the liquor. About a quarter of the bottle was gone. I then went to the icebox and found the remaining two beers behind the milk. I hid all of it in the cupboard underneath the sink. If my grandmother went looking here for it, she'd have to lie on her stomach and reach all the way to the back.

At 12:30 a.m. I called it a night. I'd witnessed no activity to report to Reuven Rosenfeld. His shop and inventory was safe for another day.

It felt good to crawl between the sheets that night. The radio was now off and the two elderly women were asleep, exerting snores loud enough to bring down the roof. I had to shut their door and my own if I was ever to hope for sleep. But it was a long time in coming. I laid there going over and over in my mind the conversation I'd had with June this afternoon. Something was terribly wrong. All indications were that Eddie was faithful to Phyllis. Why did she doubt this? Why would he try to poison his wife if he were involved with no one else? Why had she thought his involvement with the military was more sinister than it really was? Surely Phyllis had known about his volunteer work at the hospital. Why hadn't she told me of it? I grew very sad at realizing I'd added to her pain when I told her about Corinne Schneider. I had told her that her husband was involved with the nurse, and it just wasn't true. It seemed a very cruel thing for me to have done, but I was genuinely mistaken. I didn't know what else to do but call her tomorrow and set things right. It was my hope that in doing that, I could ease some of her suffering.

Chapter Twenty Three

Friday, January 28, 1943 ushered in dark skies. I roused from sleep just before 8:00 A.M., but I'd thought it was much earlier because of the lack of light entering from the window. It appeared a winter storm might be brewing. Gran and her friend were still sleeping, apparently, because the house was quiet. After showering and dressing, I grabbed Helen's keys. I didn't think she would mind—I needed to get some food into this house. Leaving the ladies to their dreams, I headed out. Helen's car ran like a well-oiled machine. Thinking of my own vehicle, I wondered when I would have access to it again. What needed to be done wasn't going to be a simple task. If I was right about this approaching weather, I doubted Hep would put in a full day working on it.

The shopping didn't take long. The items on the shelves were running sparse. Only a few main staples were being put into my basket but I found myself lucky enough to be able to pick up all the ingredients needed for chili. I'd make a big pot of it when I returned home. I walked out of the grocer's $11.42 poorer. Then I headed over to Hep's station. He was in the garage with his head bent under the hood of the Chevy. I'd instructed one of his attendants to put a couple of gallons of gas in Helen's auto while I walked back to him.

"How's it coming?" I asked.

He straightened and looked to his right so he could see me. He was wiping his oil stained hands on an already filthy rag.

"Ah, Sam! It's going alright. Need another couple of days. Of course, if I have to quit early today, you'd better make that three."

****

I could smell coffee when I returned home. Gran and Helen were sitting at the kitchen table. Each had a cup of it in front of them along with a plate of toast. Neither of them had changed out of their nightgowns and they were eating in silence.

"Well, ladies, good morning!" I said, as I carried in bags of food.

Each muttered an almost inaudible greeting. I raised my eyebrows, wondering where the gaiety of last night had gone. There was a definite tension in the air. I put away the items I'd bought amidst the silence. They finally finished their toast and wordlessly took their coffees to the living room. I wanted to call the Whitaker estate, but it was only going on 10:30 and I had to remind myself that it would be an hour earlier in Chicago. Instead, I busied myself with tidying up the kitchen. I then moved into the bathroom and scrubbed the tub, sink, toilet and floor. I straightened the dining room next and pushed the sweeper over the carpet. It felt good to get these chores done. At Gran's age, she didn't do as thorough a job as she used to and I had to help out occasionally. Finally, I took out all the trash, depositing it in a bin sitting on the side of the old gray stone garage.

****

The time was nearing 1:00 when I made my call to Phyllis. I was about to hang up after the sixth ring when I heard a breathless voice on the other end.

"Mary? Is that you?"

"Oh," she said breathing heavily into the mouthpiece. "It's me, just a tad out of breath. I was comin' up the stairs when I heard the phone. I can't run like I used to."

"Well, I'd like to talk to Phyllis if I could."

"She ain't here, and not likely to be for who knows when. If I may be so forward, she comes and goes with hardly a word to us. She left for New York this mornin' and didn't say why she was goin' or when she'd be back. Augie took her to the airport and left her there. I have a dear friend who has a *relationship* with *her* employer— but not in this household. No sir, your cousin acts like we're the dirt on her shoes most times."

She paused and I said nothing. Finally, she realized maybe she'd been out of line.

"I'm sorry, Mr. Flanagan, to have been so blunt. I know it's not my place," she said stiffly.

I might have been mistaken, but I thought there was more to her anger than just Phyllis taking off. It had me puzzled.

"You have every right to your opinion and you don't need to hold back with me, Mary. You know that."

"Do ya mean that, sir?" she asked, still sounding very cool in her tone.

"Of course, I do."

"Well, then let me tell ya that ya were missed at the viewin' and service. Brigitte and I looked for ya. Ya know they buried him yesterday?"

This was not idle information. Mary was telling me I was missed because I should have been there. I wasn't and that was disrespectful. After all, in her mind, Phyllis was my cousin and Eddie was my cousin's husband. And Mary had a very fond spot in her heart for Eddie Killburn. She wasn't privy to the fact that he had tried to murder his wife. She was rebuking me. But I believed the real focal point of her discontent was now apparent. I suspected she had thought our relationship, mine and Mary's, warranted some word from me before permanently exiting her life. She was right.

"I know, Mary. I should've been there and I wanted to be, but my grandmother needed me and I had to return to Detroit. I called Monday night to tell you, but there was no answer."

I didn't need to add a false tone of sorrow into my apology; I was being sincere. Her mood softened.

"I wish ya could've seen it. The service was beautiful." Her voice was getting weepy. "The priest sayin' all those kind words and him describin' the hereafter to us. It still doesn't seem quite real."

She paused, seeming to realize for the first time what I had just said; that I was no longer in Chicago.

"Ya say you're back in Detroit?"

And then she started to cry.

****

After I'd disconnected, I still stood near the telephone in an attempt at pulling myself together. There was no conversation drifting toward me from the living room. I walked that way and stopped under the archway, which divided where the women sat from the dining room. Helen and Gran were each seated on the couch as far apart as they could possibly get. They each stared straight ahead, holding their coffee cups. I put my fists on my hips and released an over dramatic sigh.

"Okay, out with it! What's going on between you two?"

Neither of them spoke.

"Helen?"

She turned her face toward the wall.

"Gran?"

"Ask her!" my grandmother said, sharply.

"I did and she's not answering, so I'm asking you."

My grandmother made an exaggerated gesture of zipping her lips together.

"Well, you're going to have to speak some time. And until you tell me what this is about, I'm not making dinner."

I moved to one of the beige chairs that sat in the living area and sat down. I leaned forward placing my elbows on my knees and rested my chin in the palms of my hands. I stared at them and didn't deviate from that position. It worked. Ten seconds passed and my grandmother shouted out.

"She called me a liar!"

Gran pointed her forefinger at Helen.

"I most certainly did *not!*"

"Did too!"

"Well, it sure didn't jump out and walk away on its own!" Helen yelled.

"Maybe *you* took it out and put it somewhere else! And now you don't know where you put it! I wouldn't doubt that brain of yours is getting scattered in your old age!" my grandmother shouted.

"What are you talking about? I'm six years younger than *you*, dearie! I'll just go home!"

"Ladies, ladies; hold on. First of all, no one is going anywhere. Look." I pointed to the front window and they turned in their seats to see. "Look at how heavy the snow is coming down. And secondly, what exactly are we talking about here?"

Helen spoke. "I had something in my purse and now it's gone. *She* probably took it!" she said with a gesture toward Gran.

"See? I *told* her I didn't touch it and she doesn't *believe* me. She's calling me a liar!"

Laughter rose in my throat.

"You wouldn't happen to be talking about the vodka, would you?"

They both looked at me, appearing sheepish.

"*I* took it last night, Helen. I didn't want Gran passing out or you getting sick. I hid the vodka along with the beer."

They didn't say a word, but I continued.

"And you wonder why the pastor gives sermons on how destructive drinking is! Look what it's doing to your friendship." I held up my hands and shrugged. "But far be it from me to tell you two how to live your lives. You two are old enough to make your own decisions."

I got up from where I was sitting and told them to follow me; I needed their help making the chili. As they walked behind me, I was listening to their conversation.

"He's right. That was silly of us. We'll just have a drink with the chili. You got more orange juice?" Helen asked.

I rolled my eyes. *Oh brother!* I thought.

"Yeah, but I don't like that hard stuff. I'll stick with the beer. That vodka stuff tastes like kerosene. We just won't get drunk."

I stopped in my tracks and turned around.

"What did you say, Gran?"

"I said we won't get drunk."

I could hardly wait for dinner to be over and the kitchen to be cleaned up. The women were sitting in the dining room now, listening to some show on the radio. I searched for paper and a pencil. Now I could sort out what I'd been thinking ever since the ladies had made amends. Once seated at the kitchen table, I listed each and every person who had given me information, or anyone who might be connected to the Killburn case. On paper, I headed columns with the names of the players, so to speak. Under their names, I wrote what I'd learned from them and how they were connected, and anything, no matter how trivial, that they'd said. For instance, today, Mary had told me that Phyllis went to New York. I remembered Brigitte had come up to Phyllis at the party and told her she'd had a call from there; but whoever it was said they would call back later. I kept writing

211

incidentals under the proper heading and cross-referencing them. If I was to find what really happened to Eddie Killburn and why, I'd need more information. The theory was that Eddie had tried to poison Phyllis, but mistakenly drank it himself. But *why*? I was ready to believe that he wasn't involved with anyone else. What could have been his motive then? Unless cashing in on the large insurance policy he'd taken out on her had been his sole intent. Not one person gave me the impression that Eddie was motivated by greed. Eddie, himself, didn't give me that impression. In fact, now knowing of his volunteer work and the recreational room he'd provided at the hospital, it appeared that he was very generous with his time *and* money. I'd seen Dabney Harrell and Ted Brock enter the room where Eddie was playing the piano shortly before his death. Could either one of them have slipped something into that drink? I now thought I knew the answer, but I wanted to make sure. If what I was thinking was correct, I'd been a damn fool!

I kept looking at the clock. I wanted to call Harry at a time when I could catch him at home. I didn't remember the number at the Trib, but I had his phone number at the house written down. I needed his help in proving I was correct with my suspicions.

After a couple of hours, I rose and stretched. My legs were getting achy from sitting in one position for so long. I passed through the dining room and noticed the old gals were growing sleepy; Helen with her orange juice and vodka, Gran with her beer. I entered the living room to gaze out onto the street. Snow was still falling, and it had been building up at a rapid pace on the ground. The accumulation must've added up to a foot or more. There would be no surveillance of the jeweler's tonight. The roads would be treacherous and they might even be impassable in some areas. Hopefully, the thief possessed my reasoning and would stay at home, himself.

I returned to the kitchen and went to the phone, which was on the wall by the back door. It was 7:45 in Chicago. Harry answered and I grew excited. He was surprised to hear my voice.

"I need you to find some things out for me," I plunged right in.

"Sure; anything," he said.

"And if this pans out the way I think it's going to, this will make one hell of a story and you can write every stinkin' word of it, my friend."

Judith White

CHAPTER TWENTY FOUR

Every couple of hours or so, I had bundled up and gone out to shovel the snow from the driveway and sidewalk. Helen's car was safely tucked away in the garage. Now the sun was shining bright and the downfall had ceased, but its aftereffects remained. We'd received two and a half feet of snow throughout yesterday and last night. I'd assumed many businesses hadn't opened their doors. Today wouldn't find me any closer to getting the Chevy repaired.

It was the third time I'd gone out to shovel that I found Albie and Bobby in their front yard playing in the *gift* that Mother Nature had dumped on us. They had placed one milk crate on top of another on the edge of their porch. They would climb up on the crates and fall backward into the white fluff that had frosted their front lawn. One minute they were there and the next the snow had swallowed them up. I smiled and waved. I found myself wanting to be a kid again. It took a while, but Albie made his way over to me.

"Got that money you owe us?" he asked.

"You aren't going to let me get away with anything, are you?"

He shook his head repeatedly and I dug in my pocket bringing out what change I had in it. I handed him two dimes and a nickel. Bobby finally arrived and stood beside me, looking at me through fogged up glasses. I handed him the only quarter I had among the coins.

"Ha ha! I got more than you!" Albie teased his brother as he turned away and started to make his way toward his house.

Bobby remained staring at me with his face all scrunched up and his hand still open, the twenty-five cents lying in the center of his gloved palm. I sighed and gave him an additional three steel pennies. I bent down and whispered in his ear.

"Now you really do have more than he does," I said. "But don't tell him."

He closed his fist tightly around the money and headed for home.

****

We reheated the chili for dinner and when I wasn't shoveling, I was inside playing cards with the ladies. They wanted to play blackjack and Helen wanted to be the dealer. I'd gotten mad when I'd caught her for the second time rummaging through the deck to find an ace to go with my grandmother's ten-point card. I rose from the dining room table and threw my hand down.

"I'm not playing this if you're gonna sit there and cheat!"

"I wasn't cheating," Helen said in a sweet voice.

"Yeah, well, I'm not blind, either!"

"Quit being such a big baby, dear. Now sit down and we'll play gin rummy," my grandmother said.

I went into the kitchen, got a glass from the cupboard near the sink, and threw a few ice cubes in it. I brought it to the dining room with me and slid it toward Helen.

"Give me some of that vodka," I said.

She just looked at me, but didn't move.

"Oh for God's sake, I'll buy you another bottle!"

She uncapped the fifth and poured me just enough to cover the ice in my glass. We played gin rummy until midnight.

After breakfast on Sunday morning, Helen and my grandmother decided to read aloud from the Bible while sitting in the living room. Since the weather prevented them from attending church, this would be their way of devoting time to worshipping the Lord. They made me join them, even though I protested. They came up with the idea that Helen and I would each read a chapter. Gran got a pass on this one because she was as blind as a bat. When it was my turn, Helen handed me the book, pointing to 1 Peter chapter 2. It dealt with turning away from sin. That finished, we were all to admit one sin we'd committed and ask for forgiveness. Helen said she was sorry she'd felt happy when Florence Biggersby broke her little finger, which made her unable to play the organ at church. Helen got to stand in for her for a few weeks.

My grandmother spoke up. "My God, that was more than ten years ago! Haven't you sinned since then?"

"Not that I know of," Helen answered.

Now it was Gran's turn to confess, and I was eager to hear what she would say. She looked up toward the ceiling, seemingly trying hard to think of something. Helen and I waited. A minute or two passed and then I opened my mouth to give her a suggestion.

"What about the other night when you got drunk?" I asked. "How about your taking up with liquor?"

She turned to me and said, "Shut up, Sam!" And then turning to Helen, she said, "I'm sorry I just spoke to my grandson in a mean way. I hope the dear Lord forgives me."

"I'm sorry I didn't see things more clearly until it was too late in the case I've been working on. I hope the Lord and Eddie Killburn can forgive me," I said, and I meant it.

****

City snow removal trucks, all two of them, must've been out during the early morning hours, because the road in front of the house looked pretty good. There were volunteer citizens who always turned out in these situations, too. If St. Aubin was clear, the main roads had to be in pretty good condition. The problem was, I now had a huge wall of snow blocking the end of my drive. I put layers of clothes on and went out to shovel. When I came back inside, I found Helen dressed. She was out of the nightgown she had worn for the last three days.

"Helen wants to go home, Sam," my grandmother said.

"Why don't you stay a couple more nights?" I offered.

My grandmother shot me a look while Helen rummaged in her purse, hunting for something. I must admit that Helen's presence was getting on my nerves, too, but I had an ulterior motive; I needed her car. I wanted to do some surveillance at the jeweler's tonight. So, instead of plotting and conniving, I just came out and told her what I needed and hoped she would go along with it.

Still searching in her handbag, she said, "Well, no one is going anywhere if I can't find my keys."

"They're on a hook in the pantry. I put them there after I did the shopping the other day," I said.

She shut her purse and rose from the chair.

"Well, let's go then," she said. "You can take me home and drop me off. I don't plan on going anywhere for a few days, anyway. I'll just take the house key off my key ring. But I expect you to replace the gasoline you use."

Wow, I didn't think she would make it that easy for me to borrow her car. Hopefully, in that amount of time, Hep would have the Chevy going again. I took her by the shoulders and bent down and kissed her on her cheek. She put a hand to where my lips had been and blushed. She wore a smile as she reached for her coat.

"While I'm out, do you need anything, Gran?" I asked.

"Do they sell beer on Sundays?"

I shook my head no.

The roads were a bit slick on that four-block jaunt to Helen's house. One of her neighbors had evidently cleared her sidewalk, driveway and porch of all snow. Before exiting the car, she turned to me.

"When you replace the gasoline, have them check the oil for me, too. And when you get Ruby's beer tomorrow, you might as well get the vodka you said you would buy me. Make it a big one like this."

I opened my door and left the car idling. I held her hand as she made it to her front door. While heading back to the running automobile, I thought about what she had just said. Now I was stuck for getting her oil if she needed any. And I would *never, ever* accept another half cup of liquor from her again if I was going to have to replace it with a whole fifth! Helen Foster was one very shrewd old buzzard!

****

I called it quits at midnight. I'd been sitting across from Reuven Rosenfeld's business long enough. No one had tried to enter. I noticed nothing out of the ordinary. There was hardly any life on the street at this hour. I'd do it all again tomorrow night.

When I arrived home, Gran was in bed sleeping—I could hear her snoring. There was no note telling me that Harry had called, but I didn't expect there would be. He'd have to get the information from the insurance company maybe tomorrow or the next day. They would not have been open on the weekend. I made myself a hot cup of tea, then headed to my bedroom carrying it and the new Raymond Chandler book, *The High Window*, which Gran had given me for Christmas over a month ago. Crawling between the sheets, I read until sleep overtook me.

CHAPTER TWENTY FIVE

On Monday night I hit pay dirt! I pulled up across the street from *Rosenfeld Jeweler's* at a quarter of ten, a little worried that I'd gotten there maybe a bit later than I should have. As cars passed me on Gratiot Avenue, I counted them—I had to occupy myself somehow. I didn't want to fall asleep before the night was out. Staking out a place or tailing someone was always hit or miss. A dark green car passed me going too fast and its tires spit dirty slush on the drivers' side of Helen's car. That was number thirty. The next auto was traveling slow from the other direction and made a right turn at the corner where the jeweler's sat. That was number thirty-one. I leaned my head back on the seat and waited for car number thirty-two to pass.

Before it came along, the overhead lights went on in the showroom of Rosenfeld's store. I straightened in my seat and grabbed my binoculars. I glanced at my watch before holding them up to my eyes. It was 11: 09 p.m. I could see a man in a dark overcoat walking throughout the store. He reached into his pocket and grabbed something. Inserting it into the back of one of the counters, he slid the glass partition aside. It must've been a key. Of medium height and medium build, he was maybe about five foot nine or ten and 180 pounds, I was guessing. I couldn't tell much more because he was still wearing his hat and coat. Reaching in the display case, he removed a piece of jewelry. From where I sat, it could've been a necklace and it glittered with what I thought were diamonds. The man eyed it carefully. Suddenly, he removed his head covering and laid it on the glass countertop next to the piece he'd taken from the display case. He grabbed something near the cash register, put it up to his right eye, and bent for a closer look at the item. It had to be one of those jeweler's magnifying glasses. The man was probably in his mid-thirties. He had black hair and he was clean-shaven. Picking up the piece of finery again, I saw him slip it into the left pocket of his overcoat. He grabbed his hat and put the eyepiece he'd used back near the register where he'd gotten it. I saw him retreat to the back of the store and the lights went out.

That last car; the one that had been traveling slowly and turned down the side street, must've been this man's auto. He must've turned into the alley behind the shop and entered through a back door. I straightened and started the car. When he reemerged onto Gratiot, I was going to follow him. I'd get an address so Reuven Rosenfeld would then know which of his employees was ripping him off. Five minutes passed. Ten minutes passed. The car in which I was sitting had been running for fifteen minutes and there was still no sign of the intruder. Well, where in the hell was he? I eased out onto Gratiot and went the way he had gone, seeing if I could spot his vehicle. But the alley behind the store was empty. Damn it! He must have pulled out and continued going down this side street. I headed for home. I was going to have to describe this guy and hope the owner would recognize him from my description. I didn't want to sit out in the cold and dark again, waiting for him to lift another valuable item from the man who gave him a paycheck.

****

I was back on Gratiot Avenue the next day, just after noon. I parked on the street and crossed to *Rosenfeld Jeweler's* and entered. A tall woman, probably in her fifties, stood behind the counter near the cash register and had her head bent, writing something in a ledger. She looked up when she heard the door open.

"Good afternoon. Can I help you?" she asked, cordially.

I scanned the showroom, noting she was the only occupant. I told her I wanted to see Reuven Rosenfeld. She asked me if she could tell him who was asking for him and I gave her my name. Heading toward the back of the store, she entered a short hallway and knocked on a door to the left. I saw her stick her head in. When she returned, she told me Mr. Rosenfeld would be out in just a moment. She was right. It didn't take him long to come out of his office and wave me back to it.

Mr. Rosenfeld was a man of average height. He was average in build; except for his gut, which hung over his belt. Gray hair hugged the sides and back of his head, and he was completely bald on top. His office was small with an expensive looking desk sitting out a bit from one wall and a really nice leather chair perched behind it. A matching couch faced his desk. I sat on it. The wall to my right had a window built into it and the curtains were drawn. My guess was that it looked out onto the alley. The wall across from the window had a couple of small shelves lining it. Books about precious gems and photos in frames sat on those shelves. I removed my hat and sat it next to me on the sofa while he returned to his chair behind his desk.

"I see I'm interrupting your lunch, sir," I said to him.

Sitting on his desk was a napkin, spread out. On the napkin sat a half-eaten egg salad sandwich, carrot sticks and pieces of green pepper. He had a glass of water beside it. He dismissed my remark with a wave of his hand.

"Oh, don't worry about that! I tried to call you at your office this morning with no luck, Mr. Flanagan. I was hit again last night. Whoever is doing this got away with a six thousand dollar necklace. I sure hope you have some news for me. I can't afford for this to go on much longer."

I told him what I had seen last night and admitted how the culprit had gotten away from me. I told him I would do my best to describe him.

"Never mind that, my friend," he said.

Rising from his chair, he walked over to his bookshelves and removed a black framed picture of a group of six people. He handed it to me.

"Just pick him out," he said. "That was taken at our annual picnic last summer. All of them are still employed here."

Holding the picture closer, I saw that all of the employees were men except for the one woman who was in the showroom now. I looked at each of them and studied their faces, wanting to make sure that when I pointed to one, it was the right man. He wasn't in the photo.

"Are you sure?" he asked me. "Look again."

I handed it back to him.

"I could look at this all day long and it wouldn't change a thing. He's not in there. You know what this means, don't you? It's gotta be a former employee. Have you fired anyone lately? Or maybe let someone go before that picture was taken? Someone maybe quit and they took the time and trouble to make a replica of the key to the store?"

He moved away from me and replaced the picture on the shelf. He returned to my side of his desk and leaned against it, scratching the top of his head.

"Well, I had a man work for me who quit a few years ago. But he moved to the west side of the state. That's the reason he left my employ; he was moving. I haven't heard he was back in town or anything, but I suppose he could be."

"Does he have black hair? Would he happen to be about five foot ten inches?" I asked him.

"Not sure on the height; could be, but the black hair is right," he responded.

Rising from the sofa and grabbing my hat, I asked for the name of this former employee, and told him I would check him out to see if he was back in town. On my way out, I made a detour to his bookshelves. Spotting a particular picture, I picked it up. It was a photo of Reuven, a much younger Reuven and a woman. He had a lot of black hair in the snapshot. He followed me and stood by my side.

"This your wife?" I asked him.

He looked down at the framed image. He smiled and nodded.

"Been married thirty eight years to her," he said.

I replaced the photo and he reached in the back, picking one up that had been obscured by others.

"Isn't she a doll? That's my granddaughter," he said, handing it to me.

I was holding a gold framed picture of a man and a woman sitting on the floor in a living room where a Christmas tree stood behind them. Gifts were under the tree and the woman was holding a beautiful three or four year old little girl on her lap. The child had dark curls circling her head.

"The whole family is good looking," I said, honestly. "Is that your daughter and her husband, or your son and his wife?" I asked.

"My son, David; I have no daughters. We have three boys. David runs the business with me now. In fact, at the end of this year, I plan on handing him the keys to the whole thing. I'm getting tired and I'd like to travel with what time me and my wife have left."

I put the photo back on the shelf and turned to Rosenfeld.

"Good thing you haven't given him the store yet," I said.

"What?" he asked.

"If it were me, he'd get nothing," I said.

"What are you talking about, and what business is it of yours?"

His tone suggested he was very offended at my brazenness; what he might call chutzpah.

"Hmm," I said. "I hate to tell you this, but he's your man."

"What?" he asked, startled.

"David is the one who's been robbing you blind. That's the guy who was in here last night."

His face paled. He asked if I was absolutely sure and I told him that I absolutely was. Leaving his office, I noticed that the door across from his own was now open. I glanced in, and the man sitting behind the desk caught the movement. He looked up and saw me peering at him. Smiling, I tipped my hat to him and continued to walk toward the front of the store to take my leave. The man was David Rosenfeld.

Maybe I'd told the jewelry storeowner what he'd already suspected and then again, maybe he didn't suspect his son at all. Either way, I walked out of Reuven Rosenfeld's store $30 richer. I went to spend some of it. I stopped at Hep's and had Helen's tank topped off. His attendant checked her oil and said it was fine. Hep gave me some good news, saying he thought my Chevy would be ready late tomorrow afternoon. He gave me some bad news when he told me what it would cost. Even with the ten percent reduction he'd given me, it was more than I wanted to spend. *Oh well*, I thought. Before going home, I made a stop at the corner store and picked up a pack of cigarettes, a six-pack of beer and a fifth of cheap vodka. Helen wasn't likely to know the difference. After that, I guided the car toward St. Aubin Street. I was done for the day.

****

Harry's call came at 8:15 that night.

"You owe me big time, buddy," he said after I'd answered the ringing instrument." Don't you ever tell Myra, but I had to take the secretary out to lunch and sweet talk her to get the information. The head guy at *Bartles and Conroy Insurance Agency* is at a week-long conference in Lancaster, Pennsylvania. I had to get the lowdown from her. Once she thought I was interested, it was easy to get her to talk. Hey, what can I say? She thought I was cute. She might not be so bad herself if she'd shed a hundred pounds and pluck some hairs out of her chin."

I laughed, "Okay, so what *is* the lowdown?"

He told me and I jotted some of what he was saying on a piece of paper.

"And," he said, "you were right on that other thing. It *was* him! But he's gone now. He went back to New York over a week ago. And, I know you didn't ask me, but I thought I'd check on Phyllis Killburn's return trip. She got in late last night."

I whistled into the mouthpiece. I told him I had to make another trip out to Chicago. I had to sit down with Phyllis and tell her what I'd found out.

"Don't worry, though," I assured Harry. "I'll get a hotel room this time. But you and I *will* be meeting after I see her so you can have the story."

"Not gonna tell me now, huh?" he asked.

"Nope!"

"Hey, Sam? You aren't staying at a *hotel*, either. I mean, I really don't care *what* you do, but Myra would have my tail if you didn't stay here. See ya soon, my friend."

"Thanks, Harry. Yep, see ya real soon."

Judith White

CHAPTER TWENTY SIX

On Wednesday morning the phone rang and Gran beat me to it. I heard her yell into the instrument.

"*Huh*? You say you want *Sam*, or did you say *Stan*?"

I quickly grabbed the receiver from her.

"Hello?"

Hep was laughing, and then he sighed.

"Ah, Sam, I gotta tell you; your grandmother is one crazy character."

"That she is, Hep. Now don't tell me you're calling to add another day to repair the Chevy?"

He wasn't. He was calling to say he'd made better time than he thought he would. The Chevy was ready now. He could have one of his boys bring it out to me if I could drop the kid back off at the shop. I told him to give me a half hour and I had him jot down Helen's address.

"I borrowed my grandmother's friend's car. Have the kid go there and I'll give him a lift back to the station and I'll come in and pay you."

"Now, Sam, if you don't have it all today, you can make payments on it. Hell, you don't even have to give me *anything* today. I can wait a week or two if that's better for you."

Like I said before, Hep was a good man, a caring man. But I assured him he would get his money, in full, when I dropped his employee off. We hung up and I went to get dressed. I drove into Helen's driveway at 10:15 a.m. I got out of the car, making sure to lock it for her. The Chevy was nowhere in sight yet. I knocked on the side door of the big house and Helen answered. She opened the screen door a crack and I told her I didn't need her car anymore, thanked her for the use of it and held the keys out to her.

"Your oil is fine and the tank is full."

I held up the brown paper bag containing her liquor.

"What's that?" she asked.

"It's your vodka."

"Oh. Thanks very much."

She grabbed it and shut the door and I heard the lock turn. I was left standing there looking like an idiot. *She could've asked me in*, I thought. Boy, was I ever right about her being a rude old buzzard at times! Pulling the collar of my coat up, and burying my hands deep in its side pockets, I walked back and forth in the drive to keep moving so as to generate some heat within my bones. Helen was at her front window, watching me. Still, she never asked me in. Still, she never stuck her head out the front door to ask how I was getting home. Relief swept over me when the kid from Hep's station pulled up in my auto. He kept the engine running and put it in park. He hopped out and ran around the front of the vehicle to the passenger side, while I slid behind the wheel. The interior was warm and it felt good. I pulled away from the curb.

"Have trouble finding the address?" I asked him.

"Yeah, must've passed the street three times before I realized this was it."

I looked at him. He appeared really young and I didn't think I'd ever seen him before. I asked him if he was new at the station.

"Yep," he nodded. "Been there since right after the holidays. Hep Cat is training me to be a mechanic."

"Well, you're learning from the best," I said.

"Don't I know it?"

"You don't look old enough to have graduated from school, though," I laughed.

"I'm not. I quit after last semester, right before Christmas. I won't be seventeen until August."

I looked over at him.

"Now what'd you go and do something like that for? You'll probably end up regretting that someday."

He shook his head and said, "Eh, I don't think so. I found school boring. The way I figure it, I can earn some pennies from heaven this way. I'm getting trained while the Hep Cat pays me. How killer-diller is that? When I turn seventeen, I wanna see if I can get into the army. This mechanic stuff might come in handy when I join, and then, I got a job waitin' for me when I get out."

Huh, pennies from heaven, I thought. Kids nowadays were always looking to make easy money. I still didn't agree with his quitting school one term before he was to graduate, but I couldn't fault him too much. He knew what he wanted and he had a plan. He started to tap his fingers on his thighs, like he was playing a tune on a set of drums. I smiled and focused my eyes on the road. The Chevy hadn't performed this smoothly in months.

****

Before I left for the Greyhound station, I asked my grandmother if she still had that money that I'd handed her when I left the last time. She said she did and that she'd hidden it. It was good that she still had it. I'm not so sure it was good that she had hidden it, and I prayed she could remember where that was. I told her I wouldn't be gone so long this time, assuring her it would only be for a few days.

"That's okay, dear. With Helen staying here so many nights, I could really use a break from the two of you," she said. "Don't worry about me."

I headed out to the auto with my overnight bag and saw Albie shoveling his drive.

"Hey," I called over. "I'm heading out of town for a few more days."

"Okay, gotcha. What's the pay this time?" he asked.

"What do you think your time is worth?"

"Dollar!" he shouted back.

I shook my head.

"Okay," he said. "Fifty cents and that's as low as I'm gonna go."

"You'll go lower and like it," I shouted back. "It's a quarter and no more. Take it or leave it."

"I'll take it!" he agreed.

I got in and started the Chevy and put it in reverse. Albie hadn't mentioned Bobby in our negotiations and for that, I was grateful.

The bus to Chicago was leaving at 1:30 p.m. I needed to make a stop before continuing on to the Greyhound station, but it was on my way and wouldn't take long, if I was lucky. I parked the Chevy at the curb in front of the hardware and went in. Right away I saw the man I wanted to talk to.

"Hi, remember me?" I asked him.

"Well, sure I do. How ya been? And how's that Luger been workin' out for ya?"

Judith White

CHAPTER TWENTY SEVEN

Harry had been waiting for me when I got off the bus from Detroit. I almost felt like I was returning home after having been away for a week. The sunshine had been long gone for the day and he drove me directly to the house where Myra had dinner waiting for us. After the meal, we talked about nothing in particular at the kitchen table over coffee. I kept watching the clock. At 8:30 I told them I was going over to see Phyllis Killburn. Harry told me to take the Plymouth; it was parked in the driveway, whereas the Model A was tucked away in the garage. I retrieved my coat from where it laid next to my friend's on the sofa and I left.

****

It was pitch black outside the Whitaker estate, but inside the lights were burning bright. The drapes were wide open and I saw Phyllis bring an almost empty bottle of red wine from behind the bar and pour the remaining contents of it into a glass that was sitting on the coffee table. Then she half sat and half fell on the sofa. She was dressed in her fancy lingerie. I looked at my watch. It was almost 9:00 p.m.

I got out of the auto and went to the door, knocking twice. The look on her face when she opened it was priceless. She was stunned that it was me.

"Sam! What are *you* doing here?"

"I need to talk to you," I said.

"I had just assumed you went back to Detroit," she said. "If this is about the money you think you need to reimburse me, well, I—"

I cut her off.

"Aren't you going to invite me in?" I asked.

"Oh, forgive me. Come in."

She moved to the side and I passed her, entering the room with the bar and the paintings, the room in which she had been sitting. She shut the door and went to her place on the couch. I stood there and removed my fedora. I gestured to the bar with it.

"Mind if I make myself a drink?"

Her face registered surprise that I would assert myself in such a way. She finally found her voice.

"No, of course not. Go right ahead."

She watched as I moved to the other side of the room. Picking up the finest scotch in her array of liquor, I chose a short glass to pour it into. I added a few cubes of ice. Where she was sitting now, I had sat the night of the party when I'd heard Brigitte's scream, causing me to spill coffee all over Harry's tuxedo. I went to sit across from her in a green chair whose back was to the window. The coffee table was between us. I took a taste of my drink and held it up, telling her the scotch was excellent.

She watched me carefully. She was trying to figure out what the reason for my visit was. Finally, she spoke.

"I don't understand, Sam. What is it you have to tell me?"

"How was your trip to New York?" I asked. "I called but Mary said you'd flown out that morning. What was in New York?"

She seemed to relax somewhat and she sipped at her wine. She took a cigarette from her gold case and lit it. After inhaling and exhaling, she looked at me.

"Nothing in particular, I guess. Anywhere would've done. I needed to get away. The stress of the past week has been horrendous. I miss him so much, Sam."

"Who do you miss, Phyllis?"

She looked at me, taken aback, but said nothing. She finished off her wine and I took another sip of my drink.

Gesturing toward her empty glass, I asked, "Can I get you another drink, Phyllis? I can make you a martini, if you'd like."

"Oh no, I don't...uh...I think there's another bottle of wine back there. I can get it."

She rose and disappeared behind the bar, and I watched as she uncorked it and brought the bottle back with her. Her walk was slightly unsteady. She refilled her glass, setting the new bottle next to it, and picked her cigarette up from the ashtray.

"What were you going to say? You don't what?" I asked her.

Her look was guarded and she squinted at me with her eyes. I continued.

"You don't like hard liquor?" I provided her with the answer. "Is that what you were going to say? You told me that once before. The first time I was in this house. You told me it tasted like poison to you. My grandmother, of all people, reminded me of your comment. Just this week she said she didn't like the hard stuff because it tasted like kerosene. Only you used the word poison. You said it was like poison to you. So tell me sister, how in the hell could Eddie have made a martini for you when he knew you didn't drink vodka or gin? So let me ask you once again. Who do you miss, Phyllis?"

Her eyes grew a bit wider and the color rose in her cheeks. I pushed ahead.

"Let me tell you a little story. You came to Detroit to find a P.I.—anyone would do, I just happened to be the lucky guy. I was your patsy. You had the whole con worked out in your mind. You needed someone to back up your suspicions about Eddie to your friend O'Bannon, and I was that someone. But you needed this someone to be from out of town; someone who would go back to where he came from and never dig any further into your husband's death, and Detroit was just far enough away to fit in with your scheme. I wondered why you insisted that I attend the dinner party. You needed me there; you wanted me to stick around for the finale so I could give my account to the police about your hiring me, your suspicions, and Eddie's drunken threats. There was a definite method to your madness, Phyllis. I'll give you that. The only thing is, I don't like being used."

She stubbed out her cigarette and glared at me.

"This has gone on far enough! I want you out of my house immediately. If you don't go, I'll call the police!"

"Oh, we'll call them, believe me. But in just a bit. First, I want to go on with my tale. Now I may not have *all* the facts straight, but pretty much."

She started to rise from the sofa, but fell back onto it. She appeared to have had a tad too much to drink, and it seemed to be messing with her coordination. I went on.

"You know, it's funny. Most people wondered why Eddie married you. In our minds, we thought he might tire of you, and so it was plausible he might have wandering eyes for a younger woman. With his looks, he could've gotten anyone he'd wanted. We never thought it might be the other way around; that you would want to get rid of him."

I looked past her and focused on the painting of the English countryside. I recalled what he'd said to me while I was looking at it. He loved the painting Phyllis had given him as a wedding gift, and he told me she'd always known what he loved. Eddie really did love Phyllis, just as Charlie Kuntz believed.

"Let me try this one on you. Back in, say, early November of last year, you met up with Jack Calvert again. Someone told me he'd heard a rumor that Jack had returned to Chicago. That rumor was fact. I don't know if he called you, or maybe you just ran into him somewhere in the city. You talked. I don't know why he came back to Chicago and stayed so long; maybe it was business, who knows? You arranged to see him on occasion. All the old feelings surfaced. Maybe it was just a bit of flirtatious fun with him, but it wasn't with you. After all,

you had loved this man with all your heart and soul.
Now, maybe you *were* truly fond of Eddie at one time—I
don't know; maybe you weren't. But Jack Calvert was
the *real* love of your life. You had never *stopped* loving
him, and now that he was back in town, you wanted to
make sure he stayed here. You had plans for the two of
you, and Eddie was in the way. The night of the party,
you found out that Jack had returned to New York. You
knew it because Brigitte told you someone called from
New York and he said he'd call later, not wanting to
interrupt your get-together. You put two and two
together, knowing it was Jack. He had left you again.
You had no idea he was planning on leaving—he hadn't
told you. And you had no idea he would be leaving you
behind. But he did, and that really unnerved you. Those
tears for Eddie were actually for Jack Calvert. That really
worked in your favor, Jack leaving like he did. Those
tears were genuine. I thought they were for Eddie; you
had me fooled. I remember you saying something like '*I
trusted him. How could he leave me?*' I thought it was a
bit odd, but then again, your husband had just died and
it's normal to be distraught under those circumstances.
But those tears weren't *for* Eddie. They were about Jack
going back to New York and not telling you; not wanting
to take you with him."

Anger rose from deep within her. Her face
transformed into something ugly.

"You don't know *anything*!" she shouted.

"I know that Eddie wasn't seeing anyone else," I
said, and put my hand up. "But please, don't interrupt.
Let me go on with this and let's see what I know. You

came to Detroit and gave me a load of bull about not knowing what your husband's connection with the military was." I started to laugh. "What? Was that something you'd just thought up while sitting in my office to make it more interesting, to make Eddie appear more sinister? More like the bad guy? You knew *exactly* what Eddie's volunteer work was all about. You knew about Corinne Schneider the whole time. You knew how Eddie was helping her husband. He was probably the type to come home each night and share everything with you."

"This is ridiculous!" she said. "Even if what you say is true about Jack, I could've divorced Eddie. Why would I want to kill him?"

"Now here's where it gets really interesting," I said. "In order for Jack Calvert to marry you again, your husband had to be dead. You couldn't divorce him."

"And why not? Oh, you're making no sense! I didn't kill Eddie!"

"Oh yes you did! And you're going to pay for it, sister! Jack would never go against his faith and marry a divorced woman. His church doesn't allow it, and he follows the guidelines of the Church to a tee!" I shouted. "In fact, he never divorced *you*!"

I didn't actually know this for sure, but it made sense and I played my hunch. It was Charlie Kuntz, Editor in Chief of the Chicago Tribune, who'd told me how Jack Calvert felt about his faith and the Catholic Church. I had remembered the conversations I'd had with Harry and Charlie about Phyllis's marriage to Jack Calvert. Harry had said something like "Daddy made sure it ended".

Charlie had used the term '*separation*'. Neither of them said the couple had *divorced*. Phyllis and Jack *hadn't* divorced, I figured. He probably obtained an annulment from the Church so he would remain in good standing with the Catholic faith. Even if he had wanted to, Jack wouldn't marry Phyllis, not if her ex-husband were still alive. But he *could* marry her if her husband had *died*. I doubted that it was Jack's intent to get back together with Phyllis, though—it was all in Phyllis's imagination. It's what *she* wanted, and he had no part in any of her deviousness.

"You're out of your mind!" she said.

I held up my hand to stop her from going on.

"I told you not to interrupt. After seeing Jack a few times and hatching this idea to get husband number two out of the way, I figure the idea of money came to mind. Having more of it would entice Jack, if nothing else would. After all, you were running on the low side. When Daddy died, you went on a wild spending spree. You were getting to the point where you found it difficult to pay what you owed. And the monthly allowance that your father had left you wasn't enough for *you*. Would it be enough to hold onto Jack?" I laughed, "Nah, not a chance."

I thought back to Delbert's outburst at *Violet Hour*. She was probably so far behind in paying for her elaborate dinner parties that they had to cut her off from having them there altogether.

"So, in early December, Eddie took out a huge insurance policy on you at *your* urging. It would be a nice addition to the evidence that he had tried to poison you. But, at the same time, the company wrote an even *larger* policy on *him*, naming you as his beneficiary. And, I mean, come on, Phyllis...how easy is it to press your colored lips lightly to a martini glass and make it look like you'd been drinking out of it? *You* were mixing that special drink for *him* when I approached you at the bar. How am I doing so far? And, just to satisfy my own curiosity; are you back from New York so soon because Jack doesn't want you, regardless? What, didn't he tell you he had a wife and a couple of kids back in New York when he was here?"

I was guessing about the wife and kids, too, but my words stung her pretty badly. She flinched and I could see the pain in her eyes. I sat back and picked up my glass of scotch. As I took a drink, Phyllis emitted an eerie laugh.

"You can't prove any of this. You're such a fool. No one will ever believe you. O'Bannon won't believe you. You have no proof!"

She picked up her gold cigarette case and found it empty. I patted the pocket of my pants.

"Oh, but I *do* have proof," I said. "I have a sworn statement right here saying that you purchased paint remover from the *Handy Hardware* on January twelfth of this year, along with a German Luger." I shrugged. "I guess you picked up the Luger as a backup plan when you noticed the hardware dabbled in firearms. I gotta give it to you; you must've done your homework. Paint remover contains a chemical called methyl alcohol. Very deadly stuff, Phyllis. And when put in liquor, you can't taste the difference. I guess you needed to buy *that* anywhere but Chicago, also."

I was lying about the sworn statement, but she didn't know that. The owner hadn't given me any such thing, but he *had* told me she purchased the paint remover and then spied the gun display. I thought telling her I had the paper made for a good effect. I could see her body stiffen slightly. She knew she wouldn't be getting out of this one.

"I need a cigarette," she said dully.

I thought I'd let her have one last smoke as I dialed Chicago's finest. She rose from her seat, moved toward an end table, and opened the drawer. I belted back the rest of my scotch and set the glass on the table. When I looked up, I didn't like what I saw. Phyllis Killburn was pointing her Luger right at my head.

CHAPTER TWENTY EIGHT

I slowly stood up. *This* I hadn't counted on. How would I know she'd kept the damn thing in this room? I figured she'd had it tucked away in one of her dresser drawers upstairs in her bedroom. Now you see? This was the kind of thing that tended to make me crotchety. Usually, I didn't take kindly to having the barrel of a gun aimed at me. Someone could get hurt under those circumstances, namely me. I didn't like the prospect of that.

"What good is killing me going to do you?" I asked. "How are you going to explain my death away? It won't look good on your resume, Phyllis, believe me."

"I won't have to explain a thing," she said. "Maybe your body will never be found."

"How are you going to pull that one off? You'd need help for that one, wouldn't you?"

As soon as I'd said it, her plan came flooding into my mind. There was always Augie. I hoped I hadn't given her any ideas with that stupid comment of mine. If I did, I was in bigger trouble than I had first thought.

Her lips slowly curled into a smile. She radiated pure evil. I didn't doubt for a moment now that she could end my life as ruthlessly as she did her own husbands.

As if on cue, I heard the back door to the estate open and close. Someone had just entered the kitchen. She heard it, too. Her head moved slightly to the right. This was my chance. While her eyes weren't fully on me, I plunged my hand into the right pocket of my overcoat where my own Luger was. *Nothing; it wasn't there!* I brushed my left hand against the other pocket. *It wasn't there, either!* What the hell? I'd specifically put it in my coat earlier this evening. I looked down. *Oh dear Jesus*, I thought. *I am wearing Harry's coat!* I'd mistakenly picked up his coat in my rush to get to Phyllis's house. *Both* of our overcoats were lying on the sofa back at the house, and I'd put his on instead of my own!

She caught my movement and her eyes fully returned to me. She fired wildly, but missed by a long shot. I ducked and something foreign and unrecognizable escaped my lips. In her condition from all the wine, I was afraid she'd have a hair-trigger finger while holding the weapon. I looked to the doorway leading to the kitchen as Augie came running in at the sound of the shot. He looked from Phyllis to me and back to Phyllis again. He saw the gun she was holding and looked up at me again, trying to put it all together. I was in a deeper pickle than I had ever been before. Oh dear God; I would never be able to take him if it came to that. I was going to die, either by a bullet or by the hands of this huge lug. He took orders and he didn't question them. He was going to help her to do her dirty work.

It's amazing what can enter your mind in a matter of seconds. All sorts of weird and maybe trivial thoughts flooded me. I thought of Gran back home. I'd left her only twenty dollars and brought the rest with me. How stupid was that? With me not existing on this earth anymore, how was she going to be taken care of? I thought of Albie and Bobby next door. I'd never see them grow up, and Albie would never get his additional quarter. He'd think I was a rat who had stiffed him, and I wouldn't be around to explain why. I thought of the Plymouth parked outside. Would they ditch the car, along with my body, never to be found? Harry would be reduced to driving the Model A. And poor Harry, he'd never get that exclusive I'd promised him.

"What's goin' on here, Mrs.?" Augie asked in his witless monotone.

She kept her eyes trained on me, but spoke to him out of the corner of her mouth.

"Get out of here, Augie. I'll call you when I need you."

His eyebrows came together in a frown. He didn't understand fully what was happening. He spoke again.

"But Mrs., what you gonna do?"

I felt a glimmer of hope and said a silent prayer to Jesus, Himself.

"She killed Eddie, and now she's gonna shoot *me* dead, Augie. She's gonna kill me and use you to dump me in the lake! *That's* what she's gonna do! She's not worth you going to the pen for the rest of your life. Do what's right, for God's sake!"

"Shut up!" she yelled, waving the gun around.

"No, Mrs. You can't do dat."

He made a move toward her and she sensed his approach. She turned to him and fired off another shot, hitting him in the knee. This seemed to throw her off balance mentally, and she let out a scream; she couldn't believe she'd actually shot him. I took the opportunity I had been given by the grace of God and lunged forward, grabbing her right wrist with my left hand. She struggled, and she was exerting a strength I didn't think she possessed. The gun went off again, making its mark high in the wall. I did the only thing I knew to do. I made a tight fist with my right hand, pulled way back and let her have it with all the force I could muster, punching her right square in the face. I heard something crack and she went down like a limp rag doll. She was out. She bounced off the edge of the sofa, landing in a sitting position on the floor with her head resting back against one of the cushions. Blood was running from her nose. I kicked the Luger to the corner of the room by the door. It was only then that Mary came out from her quarters, her eyes filled with sleep. When she saw the grisly scene, she gasped and said something about the saints in heaven.

"Call the police and ask for Kotarski and Walsh!" I yelled.

I didn't have to tell her twice. I turned my attention to Augie, who was down on his rear, holding his right kneecap close to his chest and rocking back and forth. Blood was oozing from in between his fingers, and he kept repeating the same phrase over and over again.

"She shot me! She shot me, Mr. Flanagan! Da Mrs. shot me!"

I squatted down next to him and placed my hand on his back, alternately rubbing it and patting it.

"I know, Augie, I know. You're going to be alright. Just hang on, help is coming," I said in my most soothing tone.

What he did next more than surprised me. He leaned into me and cried like a baby.

****

Mary had the smarts to request an ambulance when she'd summoned the police. By the time they arrived, Phyllis's nose was three times its normal size and it was leaning off to the right side of her face. I'd done a fine job of breaking it for her. I was rather proud of myself.

I didn't make it back to the house on E. Oakland until half past midnight. Myra was in bed, but Harry was wide-awake and waiting for me. My friend listened to the whole story, from start to finish. He hung onto my every word. As soon as I finished he grabbed his coat and told me to tell Myra when she woke in the morning that he would be at the Trib. He had to get this story out for the morning edition. When he left, I searched in the cupboards and found his scotch. Pouring myself more than I should have, I took it into the living room. Sitting back in the chair, I sipped on it and smoked cigarettes. My eyes traveled toward heaven, and I silently apologized to Eddie Killburn for the part I had played in getting him killed. I held my glass up in tribute to him.

"But we got her, Eddie. She won't get away with it. Now maybe you can rest in peace. She isn't half the person you were, buddy! Not by a long shot!" I whispered.

I laid my head against the back of the chair and smiled.

CHAPTER TWENTY NINE

Five weeks and two days had passed since the arrest of Phyllis Killburn. It was now Friday March 12, 1943 and I sat at the desk in my cramped office gazing down on Woodward Avenue. The sun shone brightly and the temperature was abnormally warm for this time of year. But that didn't mean anything. Knowing Michigan's weather, I could wake up tomorrow and see a blizzard raging outside my window.

I'd only had one case since returning from Chicago. That one took me all of three hours to solve. I'd been hired by an old woman who heard noises coming from outside her home in the wee hours of the morning on a couple of occasions. One of those times, she woke to find animal feces placed on her front porch. The next time, she found that the ladder she stored in her garage was missing some rungs. I'd been lucky on my first night of surveillance. If she had looked out the window at the time she'd heard the noise, she would've seen her next door neighbor's teenaged son and two of his best buddies running away after doing damage. This time, they'd broken out one of the back windows of her new automobile. I called the police for her. I thought my time, effort and success should net me a five spot. She told me she would pay me in a week's time. That was three weeks ago and I hadn't seen a penny of it. My client was Helen Foster, my grandmother's friend. I wasn't too worried about the lost money if she never paid me. I never returned one red cent to Phyllis Killburn. I figured I deserved all that extra money. On top of that, I collected a reward of fifty dollars from *Bartles and Conroy Insurance Agency* for saving them the painful task of making good on a million dollar policy. Still, though, Helen Foster was nothing but a conniving and cheap old buzzard.

Two days ago, I'd received a letter from Myra at the house. Of course, Gran made me read it to her five or six times. She liked getting letters, even though this one wasn't specifically addressed to her. The baby had arrived early, making its entry into this world on March 3 at 5:07 a.m. That was a good date. It had been my father's birthday. It was a girl. They named her Annie Elizabeth Blevins at Myra's insistence. She'd told me that Harry was so attentive and protective of her and little Annie that he was getting on her nerves.

I was thinking less and less of the players who I'd met while working on the Killburn case. Mary, Augie, Brigitte, Turk, Ginny and Lou; no doubt they all went on to another chapter in their lives. I'd wondered about Corinne and Artie Schneider and prayed for their success in the healing of their wounds. But I was thinking of them less and less, too. I'd probably always think of

Eddie now and then, and wonder in which direction his life would've gone had it not been ended all too early for him. Phyllis, I could barely stomach thinking of.

I opened the top drawer of my desk and threw in the rubber band I'd been twisting around my thumb and forefinger. I was going to head out for the day. It was midafternoon and nothing was likely to happen if I stayed any longer. Things were slow all over.

I was rising from my swivel chair when the door opened and Oliver Treadwell, the photographer who rented the office next to mine, stuck his head in. A lump formed in my throat as soon as I saw him. *Oh my God*, I thought, *I was supposed to hand in his rent money*! I'd completely forgotten about it, and that was well over a month ago!

"Hello, Mr. Flanagan. I hope I haven't caught you at an inopportune time."

"Uh, no, but I was just going home for the day," I said.

"Well, I won't keep you long," he said.

He didn't move into the office, but just kept his head inside the door.

"I wanted to talk to you about that envelope I'd given you before my trip to St. Louis."

"Uh, yeah, Ollie, well…uh…I think I can explain—"

He held up a stubby hand and said, "You don't need to explain anything, Mr. Flanagan. I know what happened to the money."

"You do?" I asked, feeling sweat form along my brow.

He nodded and continued, "Yes, I think I do. I never trusted him, did you?"

"Who?" I asked, thoroughly confused now.

"The superintendent of this building, of course. He seems shady to me. He always has. I think he's been pocketing rent money off and on since he started here last year. I just came to warn you about him."

He backed out of my office, closing the door as he went. *Oh brother,* I thought. I would have to find some way to replace that money, put it in an envelope and drop it in the super's office someplace where he could stumble upon it.

****

When I rounded the corner onto St. Aubin Street, I noticed an unfamiliar car parked in the driveway at the house. Maybe someone from the church was visiting Gran. I parked on the street. Gran was waiting at the door for me. She opened the screen as I approached and gestured for me to hurry up. She seemed to be anxious to tell me something.

"You have company, dear. I think he must be an old friend of yours. He seems to be a sweet young man—been telling me his life story. He says his parents live just a couple of blocks from here."

"Gran! Why do you let people in here you don't know?" I lashed out.

"He's in the kitchen, dear. He says his dream is to open up either a diner or a bakery here in town. I'm teaching him a few things. I talked him through making lasagna and he's staying for dinner. It's in the oven now."

Geez, this could've been anybody! In my line of work, I'd developed enemies over the years. I probably had enemies I knew nothing about: friends or family members of people I'd helped to send up the river. I made her get behind me and I cautiously made my way toward the kitchen. When I stuck my head around the corner, I saw Augie, all four hundred pounds of him. He was stirring something in a large mixing bowl. The big guy had one of my grandmother's aprons tucked in his belt—he was too fat for it to be tied around his waist. His head was bent over the bowl, and he was too intent on what he was doing to notice me. I backed out of the kitchen and took Gran by the arm, leading her further away, and into the dining room.

"You say this guy has been telling you his life story?" I asked in a low voice, bewildered.

"Yes," she nodded. "And what a talker! I gotta admit, though, it's pretty interesting."

"I thought you said the lasagna was in the oven? What's he making in there now?"

"I'm teaching him how to make peanut butter cookies, dear."

I straightened. Maybe it wasn't so bad to have company after all. If Augie felt comfortable talking to Gran, enough to be able to open up as he'd been doing, well, maybe that was a good thing. And she seemed to like him. She wasn't talking in her usual loud voice and she seemed coherent and normal. Yes, maybe this was a good thing, and I suddenly thought I now knew why Augie might have been on the bus from Detroit with me two months ago. Was it possible he'd been visiting his parents?

If Augie could bake a good peanut butter cookie, I just might make him a friend of mine for life. I was a sucker for peanut butter cookies. And as long as he didn't start calling my grandmother 'da Mrs.', I figured we'd all get along just fine.

ABOUT THE AUTHOR

Judith G. White holds a degree in secondary education with a major in history from Western Michigan University. She currently works part time at The Henry Ford, America's Greatest History Attraction, where her life has been enriched by meeting dignitaries, entertainment personalities and leaders in business and industry. She's traveled throughout the lower forty eight states and toured Great Britain. History, reading, playing word and trivia games and, of course, writing, is what she likes to do best. She makes her home in a southern suburb of Detroit along with her husband, Jim; two children, Brandon and Erin; and two dogs, Sadie and Orie.

Made in the USA
Charleston, SC
23 May 2012